They streamed down
Dust and smoke obscu
neighbours as you ra
covering fire, moved o
equivalent of the cavalry charge,
of the thin red line, the steady, mechanical, barnstorming assault protected by a constant curtain
of fire. Any enemy who raised his head must have
it blown from his shoulders. Here was the intoxicating thrill of battle which, in the real thing
at least, must be replaced by the horror of defeat,
the brutal facts of victory. There was Dave
yelling, 'This is bloody fantastic!' There was
Vinny, beaming all over his face, going too fast,
damn it. . .

'Slow down, you bastard!' Paddy roared above
the gunfire, but Vinny had lost it, was way ahead
as the rest of the line went down. 'Vinny, get
down!' Paddy yelled, 'Get down, get down!'

Then Midnight was off after him, Paddy up on
one knee in hope that he could bring the rogue
cog back into place in the machine, and suddenly
a geyser spurted from the dry earth and the shock
waves knocked Paddy back and the explosion
came to the ears, as it always did, after the
damage was done.

Executive Producer: Ted Childs
Associate Producer: Ann Tricklebank
Producer: Christopher Neame
Directors: Sarah Hellings, Suri Krishnamma,
Rodney Bennett, Anthony Garner, Jan Sargent,
Michael Brayshaw, Ian Mune
Writers: Heidi Thomas, Sam Snape, Victoria
Taylor, Julian Jones, Peter Barwood, Bill
Gallagher, Roy MacGregor, Billy Hamon, Jesse
Carr-Martingdale

SOLDIER SOLDIER

ABSENT FRIENDS

Kit Daniel

CENTRAL

BOXTREE

First published in the UK in 1996 by
Boxtree Limited,
Broadwall House, 21 Broadwall, London, SE1 9PL

ISBN: 0 7522 0225 1

Cover design by Shoot That Tiger!

Photographs © Carlton UK Television Ltd 1995

Cover photographs by Oliver Upton/Carlton UK Television
show/Robson Green as Dave Tucker, Gary Love as Tony Wilton,
Jerome Flynn as Paddy Garvey and Holly Aird as Nancy Garvey.

Typeset by SX Composing DTP
Printed and bound in Great Britain by
Cox & Wyman Ltd., Reading, Berkshire

A CIP catalogue entry for this book is available from the
British Library

Chapter 1

'Dave was well out of order, though, love,' Sheena told her reflection in the plate glass. Beneath her, a rust-spattered freighter boomed as it shoved its way out into the bay. It was half past ten in the morning. Hong Kong harbour had been about its business for hours.

In dungarees and with the inevitable accessory of a matching child on her hip, Donna screwed up her nose to consider this self-evident statement. 'Maybe,' she said at last. She sighed. 'Nah, but what do I want to lecture him for when he's pissed?' She rolled her eyes skyward. 'So he's on leave, he downs a few. Night before 'e leaves, out of 'is tree, I got to blaze away at 'im. I shouldna done it.'

'Yeah,' Sheena swivelled. She crossed her arms and ankles and leaned back against the windows. 'But if my Vinny had said something like that – that he wished he'd never married me – well, I don't know what I would have done.'

'Yeah, but your Vinny wouldn't have said it, would he?' Donna tossed her head. A trace of a sneer tugged at her upper lip. 'Love's young

1

bloody dream. I don't know. No, but that's what's so barmy. Night before Dave leaves, what I *want's* to stash up some memories, make sure I can't walk straight for a week, right? But what do I do, every bloody time? I get all uptight and unhappy and blow it. I don't know. It just gets so bleeding frustrating is all.'

'That's this crazy life out here for you,' Sheena nodded. 'Frustration. I don't mean sexual. Well, that too, of course,' she squirmed, 'but. . . No, I mean, they train racehorses on the rooves of these places. You believe that? Round and round in circles, poor buggers, on a treadmill. I saw a programme on the telly. High-rise cemeteries in America. Cram 'em in, one on top of the other. That's what this place reminds me of.'

Donna placed one cup and saucer on the smoked-glass table with a clatter. She took the other to the mantel above the gas fire. She yapped, 'No!' to the child in her arms. She prised her necklace from his clamlike grip. She straightened. 'There. Shut up, you.' She poked her son's nose. 'Ah, it's all right, I suppose. I mean, like, it's got its compensations.'

'Yeah. Home comforts, OK. 'Snot bad, I suppose. I mean, you're used to barrack life. My first time. Well, foreign posting, any road. This ain't bad. Pictures, furniture, all that. Cushy enough. No, I suppose, you know, it's great, havin' the other regiment wives about – you, Nancy...'

'Shortage of privacy, you mean?'

'Shortage? Jesus!' Sheena slapped her brow as she sank into the sofa. 'What shortage? Privacy's non-existent here. Guys are back, every bloody flat in the place is rocking like we've got an earth tremor. Guys are away, we depend on one another. No. No. All very well. Dave comes back, he needs a few jars, sure. Poor old Dave. But what about us? Night after night, going to bed with nowt but a teddy bear and a mug of Horlicks? God, Donna, I'm nineteen. Out there, there's a city famous for vice. It's hot. I'm not. My man's off in bloody New Zealand playing bang-bangs.'

'And mine, love,' Donna grinned. 'Mind,' she purred, 'I've talked to girls back in the UK as says they're jealous of us. Few years, it'd take a six-teen-year-old boy under the bed and a set of jump-leads. At least we don't have that problem, eh?'

'No, but...'

'Even if Dave, when he's had a few, says I'm not interested in him since I had Macaulay.'

'He never...' Sheena sank into the sofa.

'He did.'

'I'd have clocked him one. I really would.'

'I did,' said Donna simply. 'Why d'you think we're not speaking?'

3

Sheena stirred her coffee. She threw down her spoon and leaned back to stretch. Donna laid young Macaulay down on the goatskin before the fire. She looked at the pretty young brunette on the sofa. Sheena's hips had not been expanded by childbirth, nor her legs by bearing. For a bare second, Donna felt resentment, then she smiled. Sheena was a nice little chit, but boy, did she have a deal to learn. Her time would come.

'Ee,' Donna said. She picked up her cup. 'We've all got reasons to complain. Had a feller once. Used to fish on the Crocket when there were no fish in it. Dreamer – nutter, more like – like all my fellers. He used to say, "Farmers want rain on this field, sunshine on that; fishermen want rain yesterday and tomorrow, not today. They both whinge for a living." Soldiers' wives, too, I reckon. It's what keeps us going. Eh, Mam. . .' She turned as the flat's door swung inward to disgorge a shapeless mound of glittering colour. 'How're you doing?'

The mound dissolved. It crumbled. Gold and scarlet and green tumbled and flowed across the carpet like lava. At last, all that remained of the original mountain was one woman with stained mahogany hair.

Her lower contours were as brilliant as the parcels and bags which had just streamed from her. Mrs Deeley, Donna's mother, had learned nothing from her son-in-law of the craft of camouflage. Her dress – a rayon print – might have been camouflaged on the Fifth of November. Even then, her starburst gold and coral earrings would have occasioned oohs and ahs, and tears from the more sensitive children.

Mrs Deeley reeled around the sofa's arm and sprawled on it. The sofa sighed.

'Well?' Sheena turned to her, 'So what do you think of Hong Kong so far, Mrs Deeley?'

'Well, it knocks spots off the Metro Centre. I'll give it that. All this and I'm nowhere near spent up. Hello, chuck,' she crooned to Macaulay. She kicked off her shoes and flexed her stockinged feet. 'Ooh, but the heat. Look at them!' she pointed, 'They're so swollen up with this heat I've gone up two sizes.'

'Tough,' said Donna. 'You found some mug to bankroll you yet? Knowing her,' she told Sheena, 'she'll have some bloke gated with the second shot.'

Mrs Deeley glared. 'Ooh, the tongue on you would stop a clock.'

Donna shrugged. She walked, shoulders hunched to the window and gazed blankly out. She said nothing, eloquently.

Sheena yelped, 'No!' and grabbed her cup from Macaulay's stretching hand. She slurped. Donna did not turn. She sighed.

Mrs Deeley looked at her, then at Sheena. She tapped a vertiginously long cigarette from a pack. 'All right, pet,' she said to Donna's back, 'Come on. Give him a call.'

'That's what I said.' Sheena raised her hands and dropped them back on her thighs with a smack. Macaulay liked that idea and smacked her too.

'I can't,' Donna softly told Kowloon. 'I don't know his number.' Her head went up. 'Anyhow, he should ring me. It's our wedding anniversary on Wednesday.'

'Yeah, well, you wanted a husband on call, you should have stuck with that bloke that delivers the pop,' sighed Mrs Deeley. Twin columns of smoke jetted from her nostrils. 'Oh, well, you know what I do when I get mis.'

'Yeah. Spend someone's money. Great, only I'm skint, aren't I? Bloody King's shilling. Bloody army thinks inflation's something to do with plastic women.'

'Well, Mrs Deeley mused, 'We'll have to see about that.'

That at least made Donna turn her head for a bare split second, then, thinking better of it, she sighed more deeply than ever and resumed her study of the traffic in the bay.

It was good, after the rich and rare cocktail of

smells and the sweltering heat in Hong Kong, to be out here in the rolling hills and the cool fresh breezes of New Zealand's North Island. It was good, but it brought home to you just how soft cantonment life could make you. Paddy Garvey had breathed deep of this air first thing this morning, and pronounced it good, but, after six miles' running, he had proved to his own satisfaction that you can have too much of a good thing. The good air rasped like sandpaper on his lungs as he crested the hill at the run. Sweat trickled down his spine. Sweat plastered his fair hair on his brow. 'Christ,' he panted, 'I'm completely buggered.'

At his right, Midnight Rawlings spat and wiped his mouth on his sleeve. 'Not as buggered as young Vinny, Corp.'

Paddy swivelled around and ran backwards for a few paces. Behind him, Vinny Bowles, the newest recruit, was wheezing and reeling. His impish face was puce. 'Come on, Vinny!' Paddy chided. 'You only finished your group training two months ago. You should be fitter than the rest of us put together.'

'Staffordshire's – a bit – flatter – this. . .' Vinny gasped. 'God, look – Kiwis – already made it.'

Paddy turned back. It was true. British honour was being seriously impugned here. Above them, the New Zealand soldiers lay sprawled at the top of the hill, watching the efforts of the Fusiliers.

Sergeant Tony Wilton had seen them too. He took such things seriously. 'Come on, come on!' he chivvied. 'Move it, move it, move it!'

'What's the point?' Dave Tucker was never too short of breath for a moan. 'They've already beaten us.'

'That is the point, you fat bastard!' screamed Tony above the thudding of footfalls, the rattle of kit. 'Eighteen months in the fleshpots of Kowloon have done you lot up like kippers. Move it!'

They were running up the hill now, and needed that good air too much now to waste it in conversation. They heard all too clearly, therefore, the ragged chorus of '*The hills are alive with the Sound of Music!*' from the Kiwis above.

Dave Tucker was the first to arrive. 'Oy, Maria. You're late for chapel,' twanged one of the reclining soldiers.

'Shut it,' Dave croaked.

'Yeah, who let you in the Pommy army?' mocked the big Lance Corporal Milburn, who had shown no love for the Fusiliers since their arrival. 'Couldn't they get the Brownies, mate?'

If he had known Dave Tucker better, Milburn would have withdrawn that languorously outstretched leg as Dave passed. As it was, a boot, bearing the Geordie's full weight, ground down on his ankle.

8

Milburn hissed. He growled. He leaped to his feet. ''Ere! You!'

'Oh, sorry. Didn't see you there,' Dave smiled at the bigger man.

'Oh, yeah?' Milburn scowled. The two men squared up to one another for a second, then Milburn shoved hard at Dave's chest. Dave staggered backward. Milburn moved in on him. Dave found his feet and adopted the classic crouching stance of the streetfighter.

'Leave it, Milburn!' grunted another Kiwi with more than a touch of the Maori about him. He wrapped his arms around the lance corporal's waist and tugged him back. 'He apologized, didn't he?'

'Yeah, back off, Dave,' Paddy Garvey stepped between the two men. 'We got enough on our plates.'

'Yeah, you wouldn't want any damage done to pretty boy's face, would you?' Milburn pulled himself free of restraint.

Paddy thought for a second. He sadly shook his head. He raised both hands in a gesture of submission. Peacekeeping missions were a speciality of the British Army, but there always came a point when antagonists just had to be left to their own devices. He stepped aside.

Two soldiers were now clutching at Milburn's arms. He struggled to free himself. 'Bloody

British Grenadiers,' he snarled, 'come down here full of shit and can't even run up a hill.'

Dave sauntered over to him. 'Say that again, pal.'

'Nah, don't worry abut it, mate,' soothed the New Zealand soldier at Milburn's right hand. 'He's just on a short fuse.'

'You wouldn't dare anyway,' Milburn sneered. 'I'm the regimental boxing champion.'

Dave caught Paddy's eye. 'Ooh,' he shrilled admiringly, took one swift stride forward and loosed a brain-rattling haymaker to the Kiwi's jaw.

The men about them scrambled to their feet and formed a ring. Milburn roared and charged at Dave like a bull. He swung a hook, but Dave ducked it and swarmed in close with a flurry of body-blows. Milburn pushed Dave away and landed two quick, expert jabs to his head. Blood spurted from Dave's nose. Then they were down in the dust and the rival factions were roaring support for the respective champions.

Unsurprisingly, then, neither the two men nor their audience were aware of the jeep that bucked as it halted outside the ring. Tony Wilton saw it, however, and ran into the centre. 'Come on, Tucker, you plonker!' He placed his elbows beneath Dave's armpits, and heaved. The Kiwi sergeant stepped forward and placed his boot firmly on Milburn's chest. The dust hung like smoke in a bar.

Captain Kieran Voce pulled the crowd apart like a curtain. His face was long, thin and hawk-like at the best of times. Now he looked like an osprey at which a salmon has rashly cocked a snook. 'On any other day, gentlemen,' he intoned wearily. 'Now, back off, both of you, and shake on it.'

Dave glowered at Milburn for a moment, but it was he who first allowed a smile to draw a diamond on a face like that of a nigger minstrel caught in a rainstorm, he who first extended a hand.

'Milburn!' the man behind Kieran rapped.

Milburn did some clogged deep breathing, but obeyed orders.

'Thank you,' said Kieran smoothly. 'It's an early bath for you, Tucker. You're a guest here. Behave like one. Garvey, help him on his way.'

'Same goes for you, Milburn,' said the Kiwi colonel. 'At the double.'

'Move!' barked the sergeant. Milburn moved.

'Right,' said Kieran, 'get back to camp and get cleaned up.'

'Sorry, Sir,' Tony Wilton saluted.

Kieran returned the salute. 'On your way, Sarn't.'

'There's bound to be some tension,' said

Colonel Curry as the two columns marched down into the valley. 'Milburn's always been a hothead. He's a good enough soldier as long as he remembers to think before he acts.'

'He's met his soulmate in Tucker, then,' Kieran Voce spoke with a tolerant despair not unakin to affection.

The familiar puddering of a helicopter made both men turn, eyes narrowed. Colonel Curry pulled his binoculars from their case and raised them to his eyes. He gazed up into the pale morning sky. 'One of yours,' he said, then shouted as the noise became a clattering roar and the grass bowed before the blast. 'Your CO, you reckon?'

'Sure to be!' Kieran yelled back. 'The regular company commander's gone back to the UK with the forward party! This is my first detached command of my own! Colonel Osbourne's just here to make sure I don't make a total fool of myself.'

Both men had clambered back into the jeep. The chopper was now beneath them. 'Lucky old you,' said Curry as he threw her into gear. 'Should be fun. Better hurry if the old boy's going to have a reception worthy of his lofty rank. Hold on!'

Kieran grasped the seat. The jeep leaped.

'The old man', all of forty-three and, despite his fitness, feeling every year of it, saw the jeep bouncing down the hill beneath him. He had the briefcase in his hand and the door open even before the chopper landed. The jeep was just coming to a halt as he shouted, 'Thanks, Pete!' and jumped down. He clutched his cap as he briskly marched across to the two officers who approached him. Behind him, the 'chopper' set up another gale as it took off and banked away.

The three men exchanged salutes. Kieran said, 'The Commandant, Colonel.'

Mark Osbourne shook Curry's hand. 'How do you do? Mark Osbourne.'

'Ray Curry. Good to see you. With a battalion to get from Hong Kong to Germany, I'm surprised you've got time for us.'

'Ah, well,' Osbourne admitted. 'It's a bit of a personal indulgence if truth be told. As it's the last time the King's Fusiliers will see any kind of action, I didn't want to miss it.'

'Ah, yes,' the officers sauntered side by side towards the mess, returning salutes as they went. 'You're being merged, right?'

'Hmm.' Osbourne was grim. 'Out of existence, if we're not bloody careful.'

Curry cast a quick sympathetic glance at his fellow CO. 'Well,' he said, 'I think you'll find we've laid on quite a finale for you with this live firing exercise.'

'Most of the lads we've brought down here

haven't seen so much as a NAAFI bun thrown in anger,' Osbourne grinned, 'But, swansong or no, I'm sure we'll give your chaps a run for their money.'

'I'm counting on it. . .' He stepped up on the verandah that surrounded the HQ building. 'Yes, sergeant?'

'Sorry to bother you, sir,' said the flushed Kiwi sergeant, 'but we've. . .' the remainder of the sentence became a confidential burble.

Curry held up a halting hand. 'Hold on.' He raised his head. 'Mark, I'm sorry. Petty details of admin as per. Kieran can settle you in, show you round. We'll meet in the mess 1900 hours.'

'Splendid,' Osbourne waved away the apology. 'Thanks, Ray.'

Kieran led him along the verandah. 'So this is Ops Branch in here, officers' mess, and you're billeted here, Colonel.'

'All clear enough.' Osbourne strolled into the room and deposited the briefcase, cap and swagger-stick on the bed. He stretched. 'So, how do you like commanding a company?'

'No complaints, Colonel.'

'Good. And the men? How do you find the men?'

'Oh, they're enjoying the change. Bit of friction with the Kiwis, but there are always wind-up merchants in every corps.'

14

'Not in the King's, Kieran!'

Kieran frowned, then realized that his CO was essaying sarcasm. 'Oh, never, sir. No, they're fine. They're nervous about the future, of course.'

'Bound to be. It's a bad show. Demoralizing. I'll tell them what I know, which is not a huge amount. One of the reasons I wanted to come. I don't want A Company to feel that they've been sidelined, left out of it down here in the land of the long white cloud while their futures are decided thousands of miles away.'

'They known they can't all go on to the new regiment. It's a big worry for most of them.'

'Not for you, though, Captain,' Osbourne confided with a smile as he shepherded his junior to the door. 'Your future looks bright. Keep that to yourself for a bit, though.'

Kieran was smiling brightly as he stepped out on to the verandah, but, a moment later, he scowled. He was familiar with the syndrome. Every soldier who had seen action was familiar with it. He had survived.

It felt good for a moment only, then guilt set in.

Every branch of the army required discipline, but most officers knew the merits of a trifling flexibility in the day to day imposition of that discipline. Here in Special Investigations Branch, there could be no such flexibility. It was SIB's job to impose discipline. Everything, therefore, must be seen to be done by the book almost as though the redcaps were on parade full time. It was by the book, therefore, that Nancy Garvey marched to the doorway, left-turned, marched to the centre of the room, right-turned, stamped to attention and crisply saluted.

The man at the desk signed a document before looking up. 'Ah, Miss Garvey. Splendid,' he said. 'I have good news. Take a seat, please. Listen, now. An unexpected vacancy has come up on an SIB sergeant's course. Someone accidentally decided to start a family. I'd like you to take her place.'

It was one of those announcements like 'Mike Tyson's agreed to fight you.' Emotions were mixed.

You could see that in the involuntary twitch of pleasure and pride that tugged at Nancy's lips, the upward curve of her eyebrows at the centre, the shadow of worry that chased hard on the heels of the initial sparkle. 'Would that be in the UK, Sir?'

'Of course.'

'How long will it take, Sir?'

'Ten weeks. We would need your acceptance by the twenty-ninth.'

'But my husband's on exercises in New

16

Zealand, Sir. For six weeks. I'd have to discuss it with him. It would affect us both.'

'Yes, yes, I do appreciate that it's not an easy decision at such short notice.' Major Renton was sympathetic, but, his tone indicated, a little too busy to concern himself too deeply with accessories like husbands. 'If you carry on showing your present form, you could move right up the ladder. Perhaps even a commission in time. . .?'

'Really, Sir?' This time, the pleasure and pride were otherwise unalloyed. Nancy was delighted. 'Well, thank you, Sir. That you very much, Sir.'

Major Renton caught her smile and returned it. 'Important step, Miss Garvey. Right. Carry on.'

Nancy carried on with a nervous little grin and a bubble of excitement lodged somewhere between her solar plexus and her throat. She had to keep it down, because she rather fancied that it would emerge as a giggle or even a whoop of triumph.

The men had eaten lunch and now made the most of the few minutes of R and R and of the high sun. The habitual subjects of conversation in the ranks of the King's Fusiliers were, in order, how bloody the army was, how bloody officers were, how filthy the food was, how lovely that girl/drink/meal had been/ would be. Job was a soldier. He obeyed orders, moaned about crotch-rot, foot-rot and other indignities, but kept his eyes firmly upon his next leave, which, he was firmly convinced, would be heaven. And that was the problem with the new topic of conversation which had charted with a bullet these past few months and still stood at Number One. Certainty about fundamentals was one of the consolations of military life. The impending amalgamation threatened every sure and constant thing.

'So, I mean, does everyone get new gear, you know, like badges and all that?' Midnight was asking.

'Yeah.' Paddy sipped tea from an enamel mug. 'Depends what insignia they keep from the battalions that are merging.'

'Yeah, but we'll keep the hackle, won't we?' With surprising delicacy, Midnight smoothed the blue and white feathers on the cap in his giant hands.

'We bloody better, man,' snapped Dave Tucker. 'We're fusiliers.'

'Even that's not for certain, I'm afraid,' Paddy said sadly.

'So what happens to the regimental goat?' asked Dave.

Midnight burped. 'I think we've just eaten it, mate.'

'What happens to us is more important,'

18

piped up Vinny, echoing everyone's unspoken thoughts.

'You could get into the Guinness Book of Records, Vin,' said Dave with the reassuring tact which had frequently caused Paddy to observe that the diplomatic service had lost a right good ambassador when Dave Tucker joined the Army. 'Shortest serving soldier in the British Army. Joins the regiment one month, out on his ear the next.'

Worry flickered across Vinny's face like a hand over harp-strings. There was always the possibility that length of service would be a criterion. 'But – us squaddies – I thought we were supposed to be all right.'

'Ah, they'll always want cannon fodder, Vin,' Midnight told him. He cocked his head at Paddy and Dave. 'It's these overpaid NCOs they ought to get rid of, if you ask me.'

'Well, they're not gonna save money getting rid of us, are they?' Dave moaned. 'We get bugger all as it is.'

'Well,' Paddy stretched, flung away the dregs of his tea and jumped to his feet. A truck bounced across the grass towards them. 'We'll just have to wait and see, won't we?'

The truck stopped. Tony Wilton jumped from the cab. 'Letters, gentlemen!' he called. 'Letters!'

A few old hands made a pretence of casual

weariness as they arose and gathered round the sergeant. It wasn't much of a pretence. It was a scramble like puppies at feeding time, and little Vinny was first in there, beaming.

'Could be your P45, Vin,' said Dave out of the corner of his mouth. He wasn't a bully and he liked Vinny. It was just so irresistible. You saw a clockwork toy with a bloody great key sticking out of its back, you just had to wind it up, didn't you?

'Shut your face, Tucker,' Tony bawled. 'Corporal Canson? there you go. Right, got three here for you, Vinny Bowles. Some of these come from Honkers, some from Blighty via HK. Two for you, Corporal Garvey. . . Midnight, one for you. . .Metcalfe. . .'

Vinny was already inhaling the cherished words from the first page of a sheaf. Tony turned to climb back into the truck. Dave cleared his throat. 'Nothing from our Donna, then?'

'No, son, all gone.'

'Well. . . sod her.' Dave turned away, glumly defiant.

'Hey, Dave?' Vinny called happily after him. 'Wanna read one of mine?'

He was like that, was Vinny. He lurked. He bided his time. He got his own back in the end.

'Ah, go and boil your head,' mumbled Dave Tucker.

Chapter 2

Prompt at 1415 hours, Lieutenant Kate Butler presented herself before Mark Osbourne. She knew that hers was a forlorn cause, but felt duty-bound to keep the pressure on the authorities and to state her case. She steeled herself to the inevitable knockback, saluted and said, 'About the live firing exercise, Sir. I'd really like to take part.'

Osbourne's lips twitched in a weary little smile. He knew the rules of the games as well as she did. 'And you know perfectly well that that's not possible,' he said.

'Colonel, I feel totally useless here. All I do is push paper about!' She played a worn ace. 'If the Royal Navy can find an active role for women, surely the Army can.'

'Yes, but this isn't just running a range, Kate. It's a live firing exercise.'

Another dog-eared ace was slammed on the table. 'Colonel, statistically it can be shown that nothing could be less dangerous. There'll be safety supervisors everywhere.'

The trouble was that Osbourne could trump

every ace in the pack with a single card called 'authority'. He played it now with only mild exasperation. 'I don't make the rules, Kate,' he said, 'The Ministry of Defence does. As you know, that means no women in the front line. Where live firing is concerned, we are not an equal opportunities employer, and you knew that when you joined up. That will be all.'

'Yes, I knew it when I joined up,' thought Kate as she saluted and marched from the room, 'but I had assumed that the Army would progress a bit. Fat bloody chance.'

Kate was no radical feminist, but she railed against what she saw as the arbitrary and irrational discrimination practised by the Army. Sure, there were special qualities which a woman could bring to soldiering. A woman had certain advantages and certain disadvantages in terms of man-management, so while the want of physical strength disqualified her from some duties, in terms of stamina and wit she was the equal of any man in the regiment. She could run with a light load and a gun as well as anyone. She did so on exercises. It was nothing short of asinine that some hangover of protective gallantry forbad her involvement as soon as real bullets started to fly.

She was still seething ten minutes later. As usual when frustrated, she had made her way to the camp's gym to take it out on some iron. The iron seemed unimpressed, but Kieran Voce, on his back doing bench-presses, noticed her aggression. She and Kieran had become close friends over the past few months. They were both tall and dark, both fitness fanatics, both conscientious and eager to retain good relations, both with the men and the top brass.

'Uh, oh,' Kieran lowered the bar and swung his legs from the bench. He mopped his brow and eyes with a towel. 'On the warpath, are we?'

'No, we are not,' said Kate. 'That is precisely the problem.'

'Oh, no. You're not still on about women on the battlefield, are you?'

'Of course I am,' she raised her chin. 'It's not just a passing fad, you know, Kieran. They're already accepted here in New Zealand, and in Israel.'

'Yeah, right,' Kieran sighed. 'Look. . . Look, come on, come here.' He beckoned for her to join him on the mat. 'Right, now I'm going to show you something, and you're not going to take it the wrong way. Put your hands around my neck, OK?' She hesitated. He nodded. 'Come on. Go on. . .'

She shrugged and stood on tiptoe. She wrapped her hands around his neck. For a moment, they just stood like that, face to face like lovers, then Kieran raised his hands to her shoulders and very slowly, very deliberately, pushed her down to her knees.

'See?' he said, 'Biological fact: men are stronger than women, and, on the battlefield, that simple, unearned fact is worth something.'

Kate jumped to her feet. 'I'm going to do something. . .' she said softly, 'And you're certainly not going to take it the wrong way. . .'

She reached up and placed one hand on his shoulder, the other about his waist, as though for a dance. She raised her face to him. She came closer and closer. Her lips parted.

Suddenly Kieran felt his arse rising, saw the walls, then the floor reeling. He flailed with his hands but found no purchase. His teeth jolted together as he hit the floor, staring up at the ceiling, and Kate was kneeling over him, dusting off her hands.

'Biological fact:' she said briskly, 'Men are stupider than women, and weapons are getting lighter every year. . .' She stood. She grinned. '. . .Sir,' she added.

Back in the Ops room, Osbourne was causing more discontent.

Captain James Mercher was not a popular man. His bullish, often arrogant manner was reflected in his appearance. His head and his neck were of much the same width, and his thick dark eyebrows meshed at the centre. If Kieran or Kate sometimes took the bid to gain the confidence and friendship of the men too far, Mercher leaned a deal too far in the opposite direction, which, to his bemusement, did nothing to endear him to the other officers. He was ambitious, and owed his success more to his technological expertise than to his powers of leadership.

He sat sullen on the opposite side of Osbourne's table, and it was a reflection of his somewhat childish nature that his sullenness was evident.

'It is only for the duration of these exercises, James,' said Osbourne. 'And, as overall safety supervisor, you will basically be running the entire shooting-match. It is essential that Captain Phillips takes this opportunity to take over command of the mortar platoon.'

'But he isn't due to take command until the regiment goes to Germany,' brooded Mercher.

Osbourne could have told him to do as he was told and be done with it, but he was aware that Mercher's arrogance had nothing to do with confidence, and he wanted Mercher's commitment to be unalloyed by resentment – if possible. 'I am aware of that, James,' he said, and his tone was monitory at least, 'which is why I want him to gain experience under these conditions. Furthermore, I need someone of your calibre to keep an eye on the way Kieran Voce handled the indirect fire. It's a big first for him as acting OC.'

'With respect, Colonel Osbourne,' Mercher objected with a pout, 'that is not why I am here.'

Again Osbourne checked his first impulse. He knew better than most the true meaning of that disrespectful preamble, 'with respect'. 'James, James,' he said as though his head hurt, 'there are big changes ahead. Now, we are not going to get very far if every man-jack digs his heels in every time he's redeployed. We have got to be ready to learn new skills, co-operate within new frameworks.'

'Yes, Sir.' Mercher was sensitive enough to catch that warning. 'Adapt and survive; is that the message?'

'Something like that,' said Osbourne, who was impatient of such slogans.

But Mercher had found an interpretation which he could – as he would have said – relate to. He was not happy, but he said, 'I see. Thank you, Sir.'

'Thank you, James,' said Osbourne.

He sighed deeply as the other man left the room.

'Yeah, yeah, all right, field marshal in ten years. Great if you like that sort of thing.' Donna pressed the lift button marked 'Down'. The lift hummed somewhere way below as if wondering if it could be bothered. 'But what's Paddy gonna say about all this?'

Nancy shrugged. 'He'll be thrilled to bits.'

'You reckon?' asked Sheena. She added her persuasive stab at the lift button. It considered again.

'Can't see him being thrilled to bits when he has to salute you. Mind, useful to be able to tell him to stand to attention and get a response every time.'

'Donna!' Sheena giggled.

'Yeah, OK,' Nancy shook the worries out of her brain. 'But listen, we're not talking about a commission straight away. Nah. He'll be fine.'

The words seemed to sing in the landing walls. Nancy didn't like that. 'Oh, come on,' she sighed. She set off down the stairs.

'You'll have to speak to him, mind,' Donna called behind her. Donna's high heels made a beginners' slope into a *Ski Sunday* special. She had to cling tightly to the bannister.

'Yeah, well, I just tried.' Nancy's voice fluttered up the stairwell. 'He's uncontactable. They're out on manoeuvres.'

'Well, can't you go over and see him?' Sheena called down above the clatter. 'Just get some leave?'

'Yeah, sure, only I'm absolutely skint.'

'Snap,' said Sheena.

'Snap, bloody snap,' Donna droned.

'Stop!' It echoed down the stairwell. Maybe it was Nancy's familiarity with order, maybe it was those stilettos. Whatever, Nancy stopped dead and Donna careered into her on the landing. Sheena was more circumspect. All three girls gazed up at the apartment door.

Mrs Deeley made her way down the flight. Macaulay sucked his thumb and nestled in close to all that slithery satin. 'Look, pet,' Mrs Deeley told Donna softly, 'I can't stand seeing you with all them white roses in your cheeks.' She held out a hand stuffed with notes. 'Here, take some of these dollars. See if you can't get yourself something nice. Call it an anniversary present.'

'Oh, Mam!' Donna was all choked up, but remembered to take the money in her hands before taking her mother in her arms.

There was, then, the trace of spring in Donna's teetering steps as the girls made their way into the blizzard of sensations that was the streets of Hong Kong. Sheena believed that she would never get used to it – the way that suddenly great wafts of spicy smells engulfed you, the excited babbling of traders, the bells of the bicycle rickshaws, the horns of cars becalmed, the way you'd turn a corner to see a man holding a writhing, half-skinned snake, or you'd suddenly feel some-

28

thing soft against your calves and see a chicken running past. It was very different from Tescos.

But there again, she had to concede as she pulled down her jeans in the curtained cubicle in Modern China, an afternoon's clothes shopping delivered only gloved blows to the bank balance here. You could buy five outfits for the price of one back home. Even when, as now, she had nigh on spent the month's allowance, she could still consider the acquisition of a nice little skirt like this one as an indulgence on a par with buying a box of chocolates and a couple of magazines in Gateshead. She fastened the skirt and scooped up the tails of her shirt to knot them above her belly button. She considered her reflection in the mirror. Not bad, and Vinny would appreciate a bit of leg on his first night home. He'd get a thrill out of the daring. Donna might go about dressed, if that was the word, in dresses that could readily be interchanged with lampshades, but Sheena and Vinny were – well, a bit more conventional.

Sheena nodded. She unfastened the skirt. She heard Donna agonizing on the other side of the curtain. 'I think I've done the right thing, going for the black. What do you think, Nance?'

'Black suits you.'

'Makes you look slimmer and all. Yes. An' it goes with almost anything – white, for example.'

'Mmm. . .' Hangers scraped. Fabric puffed. 'Hey, Donna, cop a load of this. You couldn't wear a thing like that. It's obscene!'

'Move too fast, you'd poke a guy's eyes out. . . Oh, I don't know. . . It's nice, but I'm not sure I dare. . .'

Sheena pulled back the curtain and stepped out to find Donna holding first one outfit, then another up against her like a fan-dancer, whilst behind her Nancy held aloft a grotesque *bustier* that looked like a torture instrument.

'Oh, bugger co-ordinates,' Donna decided. 'Yup, I'll go for the black and the maraschino nubuck. Ah, Sheen! You might have let us see it.'

'Wouldn't want to make you *too* jealous,' Sheena grinned. She turned to the Chinaman at her right hand. 'I'll take this skirt, please.'

For the second time that day, all three girls jumped and swivelled as one. This time, it was at the vibrant boom of a gong. A red curtain had been drawn back to display a man in traditional Mandarin dress. Behind him, the gong still shivered and sang.

'What. . .?' Nancy started.

'Gor, it's J. Arthur Wong,' said Donna.

'Congratulations,' said the man with the gongstick to Sheena. 'You are our one millionth customer.'

'I am?'

30

'We would like to present you with special cer-
tificate and special prize.'

'Prize? Hey, what prize?'

'Twenty-five thousand dollar travel vouchers.'

'Way!' hooted Donna.

'Wow!' Nancy frowned.

'Twenty-five thousand. . . Whee!' Sheena
looked from one companion to the other. 'You
believe this? Twenty-five thousand Hong Kong
dollars!'

'We would like you to have photo taken,' said
the shopkeeper.

'OK,' Sheena smiled happily.

'Wearing our costume of your choice. A gift,
with our compliments.'

'You jammy cow!' Donna laughed. 'There's us
wondering if we can run to a hankie, and you just
take your pick.'

'Got to be decisive, you see?' Sheena giggled as
she was conducted down the racks. 'If you'd
made up your mind one second earlier. . .'

'Which of us is gonna hang for her, Nance?'
asked Donna fiercely. 'Or should it be a double
murder? Crime of Passion in boutique. "We just
saw red" say army wives. . .'

Sheena was still giggling as she twirled before
her two friends in a series of drop-dead outfits.
Nancy gave her views. Donna, so she said, could
not bring herself to look at these clothes which

31

should by rights have been hers. In the end, Sheena plumped for a tailored black silk suit, a frothy-fronted cream body, black silk stockings and a pair of patent courts which would have set her back a month's housekeeping. She posed for the photograph with the shop's owner and with the sales staff. She sang *I Feel Pretty* as she changed back into her everyday gear, just to keep Donna seething. As they at last left the shop, Sheena announced, 'You know what I think I'll do with them vouchers? I think I'll fly my mum out Club Class for a visit.'

She swanned on, the huge bags swinging from her hands. Behind her, in the doorway, Nancy and Donna stopped and looked at one another. 'Uh, oh,' said Donna.

Nancy shook her head. 'Uh, *uh*,' she said firmly. Both women gritted their teeth and set off after their valued friend, whom they somehow now valued more than ever.

Tony Wilton climbed wearily from the driver's seat of the Land Rover in the carpark of the Hot Lava. Paddy Garvey creaked a little as he slid from the passenger seat. Tony knew how he felt. Tony himself was whacked. It had been a long day. He was probably the fittest man in the battalion, but the unwonted exercise and the constant bawling at the men during gunnery training had taken it out of him. He was exigent with the men at the best of times, but, with a live firing exercise ahead, he had overlooked no error, however trivial. This was serious stuff.

The fresh air had hit him hard too. Had it not been for the olive-branch offered by a New Zealand sergeant who had suggested this jaunt, he'd have retired to his pit to sleep it off. In the interests of corps morale, however, Tony had sunk a quick restorative in the sergeants' mess, taken a shower as hot as he could stand then as cold as he could stand, dressed in civvies and set off with the lads to this place.

The lads who jumped down from the back on to the tarmac had donned their finery. They would have been colourful on a beach. Here, in the flush of light from the flashing neon signs, now green, now red, now purple, they were positively glorious. They strolled casually across the carpark. The throbbing beat of the bass coming from inside the club made the tarmac sizzle.

'Tasty sort of joint,' said Dave as he appraised the club.

'Bit different from the snug in the Dog and Duck,' agreed Paddy. 'Flash, like.'

'As long as the place has got beer, it can be the bloody Tower of London for all I care,' announced Tony as he pushed open the door.

The men stopped briefly on the threshold, following the military principle that time spent in reconnaissance is seldom wasted. They clocked the strobe lighting that swirled like snow in a gale around the purple walls and the mirrored ceiling. They clocked a split level room, the balustraded wooden staircases that led from one level to another. They clocked the dance-floor, up there on the right, and the long bar, complete with chrome footrail, which crowned the whole shooting match with a diadem of light and jewel-like bottles. The Kiwi soldiers were already up there, turning away from the bar with frosted glasses and frothy upper lips.

'Bar, I think' said Paddy, as though there were options. He set off for that glittering grail. 'I'm gagging for a drink, Dave.'

'Well, get 'em in, Lance Corporal, me old mucker, get 'em in!' Dave urged. He spotted Vinny's head turning as a blonde girl in slithery velvet leggings shimmered by. 'Eyes front, Fusilier Bowles. You're a married man, and anyhow, NCOs get first pick.'

'Sergeants first, Dave,' Tony corrected. 'Lance corporals get the leftovers and squaddies lose their eyesight. Now,' he smiled as he leaned over the bar, 'Hello, love. Have you got a moment? I'll have a pint of best, if you'll be so kind.'

The girl had been bending to tank the lager bottles on a lower shelf. Now she straightened, and a denim-wrapped ace of hearts sprouted a slender sinuously curving trunk in some sort of black wool with an aura. A hand arose to throw back a heavy hank of glossy dark hair. The girl turned. She grinned a thousand megawatt grin. Her eyebrows swooped like swallows' trails. Her eyes were the colour of tea. Her hair was a sort of peaty pre-Raphaelite cascade that foamed and bubbled from a point just above her ears to the points of her shoulders.

One smooth stride brought her to the bar, which meant that, if Tony looked down, he saw black. She was so close, for all the hubbub, he could hear the crackle as she unwrapped another smile. She said, 'Sure. I got a moment. You're a Pom, right?'

'That's right,' Tony cleared his throat, then said it again. 'That's right, yeah.'

'One pint coming up!'

For some strange reason, Tony's tonsils tickled. He gulped. The girl wrapped her long, fine fingers around the beer-tap. Tony gulped some more.

'Yeah. Me, I like poetry,' Dave shouted above the music. He struck a pose. '"*Twas on the good ship Venus. . .*"'

'Yeah, we know that one, thanks,' Paddy grinned, 'All soul, you.'

'I had a vocation. Missed it. By a country mile. Missed it, all the same. Couldn't get into the habit.'

'Oh, ha ha,' said Vinny. His cheeks were red, his eyes bright. 'No, it's just. . . I dunno. Poetry's like. . . It makes you feel things, think things. It's like your old style telegram, you know? It could mean twenty things.'

'Value, that,' said Dave.

'And – I don't know. It's sort of soothing and. . . All the things you feel, these guys have felt before you. Me, I can't say it. I only wrote one poem in my life, and that was on guard duty one night. It was crap. These guys, they can, though, and, you know, you read it and you say, "Right! That's what I meant to say but didn't know how." It's good.'

'Giss your poem, Vin,' Dave leaned back in his chair. 'Come on. Most poems I ever read, just a long way of saying, "Gor! sooner be in that than the King's!"'

'Yeah, but you may have noticed, Dave,' Paddy laughed. 'that your version has won you a lot more slaps than snogs. These poets get more legover per ode than you and I get for the steak, chips and brandy.'

'Nice trick,' said Dave. 'All right. Come on, Wordsworth. Let's be havin' your poem.'

'No. . .' Vinny sought refuge in his glass.

'Yeah, come on,' said Midnight, who laid his

glass of Guinness on the table with a thump. 'I like poetry myself. What was it, then? Here we go. "*How soft your lips, How blue your eyes; I'd love to get between your. . .*"'

'Thanks, Midnight,' Paddy grinned. 'That's going to get you a slug with a handbag. Come on, Vin. Let's have it.'

Vinny squirmed. 'No, it was just – you know, you're out there freezing your bollocks off, and I was looking up at the stars and thinking about – you know, how the stars are all these light years away. I mean, that star you're seeing may not still be there, right? And it just sort of popped into my head. . . No, it's rubbish.'

'Come on, Vinny!' Dave howled.

'OK. It's silly. It goes, "I am a star,
My function's to shine;
My light,
Might
Mean Something to
Somebody,
Somewhere in time."'

There was a moment's hush then. Vinny drank deep and gasped as he laid down his glass. 'There you are,' he said, 'Told you it was crap.'

'No, that's not bad,' said Paddy, and a shudder shook his shoulders. 'Not bad at all. Like you say, it makes you think.'

'Yeah,' Midnight agreed.

'Twinkle twinkle,' said Dave. 'You think, I'll drink. Your round, Vinny – or should that be Venus?'

'Oh, bloody hysterical.' Vinny scowled as he stood to gather up the glasses. His ears were crimson, but you could see that he was pleased with the reaction.

Dave watched Vinny as he walked up to the bar. 'I don't know,' he sighed, 'Bloody star. Tone's being kind of standoffish, isn't he?'

'Nah,' Paddy's head swivelled. 'I reckon he's sold on Miss New Zealand up there.'

'Yeah, seems chummy, doesn't she?'

'If I had a choice between that and Dave Tucker's company, I know which I'd choose.'

'Yeah, but Tone's not a skirt-chaser like you.'

'No, but, believe it or not, Dave, it's possible to enjoy the company of an attractive young lady without thinking of the other.'

'Yeah?' said Dave. 'Who told you that, then?'

'It wouldn't suit her, you know,' said Donna. She pulled the second bottle of wine from the fridge. God, now she knew how the guys felt when they were trying to pull. Keep the booze flowing, flatter her, tiptoe round the subject, plant the seeds of the idea, then pounce.

'Probably kill her, in fact,' opined Nancy gravely.

'My mum's a diabetic!' Sheena squealed.

'Exactly.' Donna pulled out the cork with an authoritative pop. 'Half an hour in Hong Kong and she'll fall at your feet in a fit.'

'Foaming at the mouth,' added Nancy.

'It's sweet things she's not allowed,' Sheena protested, 'not hot weather and shopping!'

'Well, I think you're out of your tree,' said Donna sadly. The wine chuckled.

'And there's nothing wrong with my marriage, thank you very much. I don't need to go and see Vinny to patch up a barnie.' Sheena's gaze slithered slyly over to Nancy, 'And I've no career worries either, Nancy Garvey. I am quite happy as I am.'

Donna stared. 'Happy? Happy?' she gaped. 'Oh, yeah, in on your own night after night with a manicure kit and a packet of ginger nuts? Bloody delirious.'

'So?' Sheena shrugged. 'So I married a soldier. I miss him, sure, but it goes with the job.'

'Aye, but you can't take domestic bliss for granted in this game,' said Nancy in her best agony-aunt coo. 'You have to work at it.'

'That's right,' Donna followed up quickly. 'You've had it easy so far. But just think. What would Vinny feel if he found out that you'd had a chance to go and see him and you didn't take it up?'

'He'd be very, very hurt,' Nancy grieved.

'Very, very hurt.'

Sheena winced.

'This is it,' Donna thought. This is the damp gusset, come-in-for-a-cup-of-coffee, will-she-won't-she moment, the moment for the direct and forceful approach.

'He might think you didn't love him,' she urged. 'Sow the first seeds of doubt in his mind, any road.'

'She's right, Sheena,' Nancy sighed, and Donna thought how good she was at the sorrowful, what-fools-we-mortals-be bit. It was positively moving. 'It really is worth considering.'

'Yeah, but I can't go all the way out there on my own!' Sheena writhed like a worm on a hook. 'I'm scared of flying, and beside there'd be no one to meet me at the airport.'

Nancy's eyes met Donna's They twinkled. Her lips curled in a small triumphant smile. Donna leaned forward and placed her hand on Sheena's forearm. 'As if we'd let you go through an experience like that on your own,' she crooned.

Sheena looked at Donna, then at Nancy. She saw their conspiratorial smiles. She sussed what they'd been at. 'You. . .' She tried to look ferocious, but the grin would not be restrained. 'You cheeky pair of mares.'

Three glasses clinked. They were on their way to New Zealand.

Chapter 3

'No, my brother was in the UK for five years,' the girl was telling Tony, 'And my dad was there in the war, but I've never been. . .' She turned as Vinny approached the bar. 'Hi,' she flashed him one of those smiles. 'Same again?'

'Yeah, please.' Vinny laid the glasses down. 'Good stuff that.'

'Get it down you, Vin. Give you strength,' said Tony, 'You'll need it tomorrow.'

'I thought it was sunbathing duties tomorrow."

'Sunstroke more like.'

'Ah, you're a cruel man, Sarn't Wilton. Hey,' Vinny leaned over to tell the girl confidentially, 'You'd better watch out for this one, Elaine.'

'Ellie,' she corrected. 'There you go.'

'Ta.' Vinny handed her the money. He made no move to leave. Of course, he had eyes for no one but his Sheena, but he liked to bask in this girl's smile.

'Shouldn't you be getting back to your friends?' said Tony.

'Oh. Right. Yup.' Vinny could take a hint. He

waved to Ellie before picking up the tankards. 'Keep the change.'

'Ooh, flash!' Tony grinned. 'Sorry about him,' he told the girl. 'Just the smell of a barmaid's apron. . .'

Ellie picked up a tray and a cloth. She lifted the flap in the bar. 'I don't wear an apron,' she said with a wicked sideways glance.

That glance sanctioned Tony's gaze to flicker down over her lean and lovely body. It sanctioned him, but he was nonetheless surprised to find his gaze doing so, and with evident hunger. The other lads might get up to a few naughties when they were away from home, but Tony had never liked or wanted that sort of thing. It was messy, and Tony liked things orderly. And anyhow, his Joy was perfect, all that a man could need. Not frivolous, no, not anyone's idea of a glamour girl, but that was what Tony valued – stability, affection, solidity. As for Ellie – well, a man could look, couldn't he? It would be unnatural not to, and a little flirtation could do no harm. 'No,' said Tony huskily.

That troublesome Kiwi Milburn was walking towards her now. He thrust three empty glasses at her. 'Three beers, love,' he said.

'You'll have to hold fire, Lenny,' she said briskly. 'I'm busy.'

'What?' Milburn's voice took on an ugly edge.

'I said, three beers, love.' He laid down the glasses on a table. He grasped those buttocks which Tony had been appreciatively eyeing a moment before. 'Come on,' Milburn muttered.

'Stop it!' Ellie pushed at his arms, but he held her firmly.

'She's just playing hard to get,' Milburn leered.

'She's not playing,' Tony said calmly. 'She asked you. Now take your hands off her, right now.' He spoke quietly enough, but his voice cut through the burble of the crowd. The other people sitting close at hand stood and shuffled away from the confrontation. Tony was vaguely aware that Midnight and Paddy Garvey had leaped up behind him. Out of the corner of his eye, he saw Dave Tucker's grin.

'Or what?' Milburn sneered. He still had his hands on the girl's arse. 'Or what, Pom?'

'Or I break both your legs,' said Tony.

'You and whose army?'

'Nah,' Paddy Garvey moved behind the New Zealander and rasped in his ear, 'He'll do it all on his tod. He's not a regimental boxing champion, my son. He's an army champion. I'll do the arms after.'

'Ah, leave us a bit,' said Midnight.

'Normal pack rules, Midnight,' Paddy droned. 'Puppies get to play with the offal.'

Milburn had released Ellie. He looked at Tony

43

where he sat on the bar-stool. Milburn was the taller and heavier man, and for a moment, the King's Fusiliers thought that he might make the biggest mistake of his life. Tone might be slight and wiry, but he was so quick that he'd have this lout tied in knots and decked within seconds.

Milburn looked around, presumably in the hope that he would find support from his compatriots. The Kiwi soldiers avoided his gaze. He scowled. 'Shit!' he sneered, then, to Ellie, 'Bitch!'

He kicked the bar-stool, just to prove that he could beat something, before striding from the bar and slamming the door.

Paddy watched him go. He turned to Tony. 'Can't let you out of our sight, can we, Sergeant Wilton?'

'Thought we were here to improve relations,' Dave taunted. 'It's diplomats like you keep us in a job.'

'No. He's trouble, that Milburn. I'll have a word with his sergeant. He'll have it in for Ellie now. Think I'll walk her home, make sure she's safe.'

'But we're off any minute, mate,' Paddy told him. 'You'll miss the ride back.'

'So?' Tony shrugged. 'I'll live. You guys go on.'

Paddy and Dave exchanged saucy glances. Paddy shrugged. 'Your funeral, mate,' he said.

*

The moon was nigh full. It cast a snail's-trail glow on the hills all around. Tony Wilton could clearly see the shapes of the camp down in the valley. He jogged towards them. When he had set off this evening, he had been tired. Now, a few drinks, one mile walk and a four mile run later, he felt ready to start a new day.

Ellie.

God, he had not felt like this since he was a teenager. It was crazy. She had eyes that you felt you could dive into, and you felt that in their depths there would be some sort of blissful oblivion. And those lips – hell, as she had said goodnight, she had been less than a foot away, and a fox leaving a limb in a gin could not find it harder than Tony had found it to pull himself back. 'Would you like a coffee?' she had said on the porch. Was she just being polite, or would he have been welcomed into her arms as much as into her house? The thought of it was agonizing, the thought of all that silky, glowing skin, the warmth of her, the scent of her. . .

But he had said, 'No. No, I don't think I will, thanks,' and they had stood there in the moonlight, saying things like 'right,' and 'night, then,' like bloody adolescents. It was just. . . If he had been one of those guys that thought nothing of infidelity, he'd have been confident and practised, he'd have had polished lines to deliver, he'd have led the dance with ease. As it was, he had no desire to be unfaithful to Joy; he had never so much as considered it. So why did he feel so happy and excited? Why did he feel so much at home when he was with Ellie? Why did he desire her proximity so?

He was at the gates of the compound now. He identified himself to the guards and, walking now, made his way around the HQ building to the tents where the Brits were billeted.

The whole thing was absurd, of course. Yes, he had volunteered to return tomorrow in order to remove the bird's nest from her porch lamp. That was only responsible. A girl like Ellie shouldn't have to stand around on her stoop fumbling with keys in pitch darkness. And he'd see her from time to time at the Hot Lava, of course. But tomorrow, in the sobering light of day, this fervour would have drained from him and he'd be back to his normal, sensible self, and she would realize that he was just a prat of a Pommy sergeant.

Tony was walking past the fronts of the tents now. It had been a long and eventful day. There was a growl. Tony's ankle was grabbed by something. His heart jumped into overdrive. Air punched at the back of his throat as he flailed, off balance, and prepared to fight whatever strange Antipodean creature this might be.

A cloud shifted. The moonlight fell on the up-turned, grinning face of Paddy Garvey.

'Jees, Paddy,' Tony raised a hand to his heart. 'You frightened the life out of me!'

'You dirty stop-out,' Paddy growled. 'So where've you been, Tone?'

'You know where I've been,' Tony was defensive,. 'I had to come all the way back on foot, didn't I?'

'Oh, aye?' Paddy's grin was bright. 'Where does she live, then? Hawaii?'

Tony looked grim. He was truculent. 'Nothing happened, all right?'

'Yeah, all right, all right,' Paddy soothed.

'Nothing happened,' Tony repeated, but he knew that it was untrue.

Chapter 4

'Ease springs, on your way,' Paddy bawled with as much urgency as if they had been under hostile fire. 'Number three, get up. Too slow, Tucker! Get down! Number four!' The soldier ran forward and threw himself down on the scrub at Paddy's feet. Paddy knelt. 'With a magazine, a full round. Load!'

The soldier fumbled with the magazine for the barest second, but clicked it into place. He sighted down the barrel.

'Ready!' Paddy shouted, and his voice came back to him from the surrounding hills. 'To your front you will see a lone tree. Enemy at base of tree. Rapid fire! Unload! Show chamber! Ease springs. On your way. Number five!'

This time it was Vinny who weaved forward at the run and flung himself flat. Paddy resumed the routine. 'With a magazine, a full round. Load!' The magazine rattled. 'Ready! Rapid fire!'

Vinny grinned as his finger hooked about the trigger. He said, 'Bang.'

This exercise was the nearest that Vinny had ever come to the real thing. He was all pepped up. Paddy eyed him with a mixture of sympathy and pity. He had been there, but the days when he thought of war as a grown-up game of cowboys and Indians were long, long gone.

'Unload! Show chamber!' he yelled with more venom that was strictly necessary. 'Ease springs! On your way!'

Colonels Osbourne and Curry watched from Curry's jeep, halfway up the hill. Kieran Voce nodded, approving, where he stood beside his own vehicle. 'I must say, it's a superb setting for a live firing exercise,' Osbourne told Ray Curry as if the New Zealander had designed the mountains and valleys with this in mind.

'Glad you approve,' said Curry with a lopsided smile. 'I think you'll find the ground pretty testing.'

'Talking of which,' Osbourne turned to call to Kieran, 'How's the round robin exercise shaping up, Kieran?'

'We've fixed it for Tuesday, like you suggested, Sir. Most of the details are in hand. It's going to be a rough challenge for all concerned.'

'Good,' said Curry. 'My boys are already seeing this as a rerun of the Rugby World Cup.'

'Ah, don't underestimate the Poms, Colonel,' Kieran warned with ardour.

'Oh, don't worry, mate. I never do.'

'Right, well, I'd better be getting back to ops

and planning more dirty tricks for Tuesday, if that's OK, Sir.'

'On you go, Kieran.'

Curry was thinking much as, beneath him, Paddy Garvey had been thinking a minute before. 'Oh, to be young again,' he sighed. He watched Kieran's jeep kicking up a wake of dust as it sped back towards camp. 'The enthusiasm, the passion. . . You come to the point where you wonder what it's all for, don't you? You never win.'

'Mmm,' Osbourne nodded. He shrugged. 'Just the fun of the game, I suppose. Just the fun of the game. . .'

Tony screwed the lamp canopy back into place. He jumped down from the stepladder and carefully laid the bird's nest on a low wall. He closed up the ladder and carried it back to the toolshed. He padlocked the shed and walked slowly back to the house. He glanced at his watch, vaguely hoping that an hour or two had passed in the last few minutes. The watch said that it was just a quarter to eleven. Tony did not have to be back on duty until two.

The trouble was that, from the moment that he had seen Ellie this morning, he had known that nothing had changed overnight. She was still beautiful. She still spoke to inner depths in him, as though she had been a figure in a dream, an ancestral ghost. She still promised pleasure and peace such as he had never before known. Although he could not wish anything so lovely gone, he almost wished that she had never been born or, at least, that their paths had never crossed. He was not a weak-willed man, but he knew that he could not withstand the force of these feelings any more than he could withstand that of the sea. He should just turn on his heel, then, and walk away. He should not go back into the house. . .

But he went back in.

And there she was, just entering the sitting-room, two steaming mugs in her hands. Jesus, when he looked at that close-textured golden skin, that long, sinuous line from her ribs to the point of her hips, the welts in those faded jeans, he felt like a man with vertigo being drawn towards the edge, knowing that the only way to relieve this pain was to fall.

'Er. . . Here's your nest.' Tony held it out at arm's length. 'Look. There's an egg inside, only it's gone cold.'

'Sit down,' she said, and her voice was music. It soothed strains that he had never known that he had.

'Er. . . Yeah. Thanks.' Tony pulled back a chair and sat. He tried a talisman against madness. He indicated the egg. 'My kid would like that.'

It did not work. She should have gasped and retreated like Dracula before a crucifix. She just said, 'Boy or girl?'

'Boy. He's a boy. Matthew.'

'Milk?' How did she do that? Was she a ventriloquist of what, that she could make her voice come from within his skull.

'Er, yes, please. Thanks. He's mad on anything to do with animals.'

She stirred her tea. The sound of the spoon on the china was strangely loud. 'I've got a daughter,' she said.

'Yeah?'

'Yeah.' She smiled a reminiscent smile that made him want to hug her and swear to be her knight errant. 'Rosa-Anna. With a hyphen.'

Tony came up with 'That's a nice name.'

'People who adopted her changed it to Carolyn,' she said, and her tone was neither self-pitying nor vengeful. It was a sound like blowing across the spout of a silver teapot. It spoke of no one emotion at source. It stimulated a hundred emotions in Tony. 'See, I had her when I was sixteen. Wasn't married.'

'Er. . .' Tony licked his lips and swallowed. 'I am.'

'Yes. Yes, I know that.' Those eyes slid sideways to tease him.

'I know you know that,' he said hoarsely.

Their eyes locked. Hell, he was a human, not a heat-seeking missile, yet he found his eyes homing in. He could not break free. It was she who turned away. 'I'll go and get a box for you to put it in,' she said, 'Keep it for Matthew.'

'Thanks,' he said, bereft without that link.

'Then we'll go for a walk, shall we?' She trailed a hand over his shoulders as she passed behind him.

His spine crawled upward like a caterpillar. Something whimpered its protest in his gut. 'Yeah. Yeah, I'd like that.'

In Hong Kong, Sheena was feeling munificent. 'Come on, Joy,' she urged, 'Whyn't you come along for the ride, then? I mean, my vouchers won't run to all four of us, but you've got the dosh. Tony'd be thrilled.'

Donna's lips twitched. She closed her eyes and prayed. She was bending to put Macaulay in the play-pen, so Joy could not see her. Joy was nice, good, industrious, censorious – a pain, basically. She'd fuss and flap and flutter like a broody mother hen throughout the trip. She'd disapprove of every swear word and interfere with every aberration, and the whole point of this trip was the odd aberration. Joy wanted to be everyone's mother. Donna, who wanted to be no one's

54

mother (much as she loved Macaulay, she'd far sooner be his grandmother), found it difficult to understand her.

Donna relaxed only when she heard Joy say, 'Oh, I couldn't. What with being marched out of here in six months' time, I've got my hands full, I can tell you.'

'Making an inventory of her pedestal mats,' murmured Donna to Nancy, who perched on the back of the settee with the telephone receiver wedged between her jawbone and her shoulder. Nancy snorted.

Joy had straight mouse hair and a serious face. She'd been starbathing. She had a galaxy of freckles sprinkled about her face. She wore a powder-blue twin-set. Her shoes were sensible. Her skirt barely allowed a privileged world a view of her lower kneecap. 'No,' she said, 'I have to take responsibility for so many of us. I'd love to go, but. . . Perhaps you'd take a present over to Tony, though. He'd like that.'

'Sure.' It was Donna's turn to be generous. 'Anything.'

'Oh,' Sheena's voice quavered, 'I hope we're doing the right thing, giving them a surprise.'

'Yeah,' said Donna.

''Course we are,' said Nancy, then, 'Hold it. Sh! What? Hold on.' She covered the receiver with her hands. 'OK, guys,' she whispered. 'They can

55

do us three seats on Tuesday. Shall we go for it?'

'Yeah!' whispered Donna.

'Go on, then,' Sheena nodded.

Nancy grinned. 'Yeah, we'll take them. First one's a Mrs Sheena Bowles. . .'

'You'll be there for your anniversary, Donna,' Sheena was grinning with excitement.

'Yeah,' Donna nodded to Macaulay. 'Long as I can get him sorted.'

'Oh, come on. I'm sure your mum'll help out. Ask her at least.'

Donna crossed her fingers and made a 'here goes' grimace.

'Well, I'll certainly help out,' cooed Joy. 'Matthew gets on with him. It's no problem.'

'Oh, Joy, you're a bloody saint, you are,' said Donna. On other occasions this might have been a sneering put-down. Today, it was a warm, sincere tribute. There were times when bloody saints were a liability. This was not one of them.

Down in New Zealand, Joy's husband was feeling anything but saintly. Guilt and apprehension made him wince as he walked with this extraordinary girl along the side of a lake. He knew what was going to happen. He could not believe his luck, could not understand why she should want him, thought that some vengeful gods must be laughing up their sleeves at him, but it was happening, and he had no more ability to resist it than a cartoon character to resist the will of his animator. It had already been written.

He still tried to steer away from intimacy with small-talk, but the small-talk had become nothing more than a soundtrack to the dialogue between their eyes, their bodies.

'It's really lovely here,' said Tony.

'Yeah,' her hand slipped into his. 'I come here a lot when I get time off.'

'Are we allowed to be here? I mean, who does it belong to?'

'Someone,' she said. She turned to face him. 'Nobody.' She moved closer. Her free hand rose to stroke his cheek. He felt her breath warm on his lips. 'I don't know,' she said. 'Does it matter?'

He gulped and said, 'No,' as those lips closed softly on his. 'No,' he breathed again, and again they kissed. 'No,' he whimpered, and his arms closed fiercely about her body and at last found relief and refuge in the darkness and warmth and moisture of her embrace.

He did not see, then, the Fusilier who passed on a bicycle on the road above, wobbled a bit at what he saw, and sped on his way with a grin on his face.

'Oh, God. . .' Tony whispered into her hair. 'Oh, God, Ellie. . .'

'There,' she said softly, 'That's that done.'

'But what about me holiday?' Mrs Deeley protested. 'Come on, Donna. I've booked an excursion into China. Lunch included,' she added significantly.

'Listen, Joy's said she'll help out the odd day. There's no problem,' said Donna briskly. 'It'll give you a chance to get to know Macaulay properly. I mean, how often do you get to see your grandson?'

Mrs Deeley eyed Macaulay. 'Ooh, I don't know. . .' she wriggled in frustration.

'Ah, look at his little face, smiling up at you!' Donna crooned. 'He knows you're his nana, don't you, chuck? Course you do! It'll be ages before you see your nana again, won't it?' Donna changed tack. 'It's me marriage, Mam, me anniversary. You wouldn't want us to go through a divorce like our Denise, would you? Come back home, bring the kids to live with you?'

That got through. Mrs Deeley's eyes widened. 'No, I bloody wouldn't.' She shuddered. 'Ee, who'd have kids?' she pouted. Her shoulders sank. 'Bloody nursemaid,' she sighed. 'I don't bloody know.'

'Yes!' Donna punched the air. 'Mam, you're an angel. Roll on Tuesday, eh? Roll on Tuesday!'

Chapter 5

And Tuesday rolled on for the soldiers with more exercises, more weapons training, more poring over maps as the round robin exercise came nearer and nearer. The King's were bent on beating the Kiwis, the Kiwis as determined to thrash the Poms, and every man worked with a will.

Milburn strengthened the British resolve with one more little joke. This time, young Vinny was the butt.

It happened during bayonet drill on Monday morning. Tony was on good form, but then, everyone in the camp knew that he was seeing that nice little Ellie down the Hot Lava. He had good reason to be on good form, from Fusilier Harding's account of what he had seen down by the lake.

'Now, just in case we've all forgotten, your other personal weapon is the bayonet!' Tony's voice pecked at the trees. 'This blade, when razor-sharp, should result in your enemy's entrails unravelling at your feet like Jack the Ripper's skipping-rope!' His spiel rose in volume and pitch to a high-pitched scream.

'Thus, Lance Corporal Tucker, a demonstration, if you please!'

For perhaps the ten thousandth time in his life, Dave hefted his weapon, screwed up his face into a snarl of pure hatred, and released a shriek of pure hatred as he charged at one of the three straw dummies that hung from the goalposts. He lunged and stabbed, thrust and twisted, all the time shrieking. It was Paddy's view that Dave had learned that banshee tone from Donna, but Dave told him that he merely had to think of all the lieutenants that he'd known and it just came naturally.

'So, Mr Bowles,' Tony shouted above the echo, 'a chance for you to impress your new sergeant with your martial ferocity!' He walked around Vinny. 'Tell me, Mr Bowles,' he bellowed in his ear, 'What's the most important thing in your life to you, eh, son?'

'Er – my mates, Sarge.'

Tony screamed again. 'Don't talk shit to me, son!'

'Um – yeah. Well, my wife, I suppose, Sarge.'

'You suppose. You suppose, Mr Bowles.' Tony resumed his stroll around Vinny. 'Well,' he bawled, 'just suppose that feller over there in the hessian hat, that bastard has just abused your darling wife, torched your domestic abode and is just about to do the same to your kids.'

Vinny swallowed. 'I haven't got any kids, Sarge.'

'OK! He's just bound and gagged your grand-mother! He's using her teeth as castanets. He has just shoved a lighted sparkler up her budgerigar's arsehole! Go! Go! Go!'

Vinny shrieked and went. Behind him, Tony continued his exhortations. 'Go! Get at him! Thrust! Kill!'

Vinny's yell very suddenly stopped. Paddy, who was watching from the sidelines, saw his jaw drop, his eyes bulge, his face pale. Paddy stepped forward, and he saw why. From the belly of the figure which Vinny had stabbed, purple and pink intestines slithered and slopped on to the dirt at his feet.

And up on the ridge, Milburn slapped his thigh and laughed like a hacksaw.

It was when they returned to the camp that day that Paddy and Dave dared to broach the delicate subject to Tony. Tony was a martinet, but he was a good soldier and an old and reliable mate. They had to give it a go. They caught up with him as he crossed the parade ground. They fell in on either side of him.

Paddy set the ball rolling. 'Look, you're gonna have to watch yourself, Tone.'

Tony stopped and turned. He tilted his chin up at Paddy. One side of his moustache twitched upward. 'Yeah? So why's that, then?'

'Oh, come on, mate.' Paddy shook his head. 'You know full well why. You know the risks. Word gets around. You know that.'

'Ah, give me a break,' Tony flapped their concerns derisively away. 'I went for a walk with her. That's it. So?'

'So,' said Dave, 'if it gets back to Honkers, the shit will hit the fan somewhat, Anthony.'

'It's Sergeant to you, Lance Corporal Tucker,' Tony snapped, then, 'Paddy, listen. I haven't touched her!'

'That may be, Tone,' Paddy cocked his head, 'but not everybody's gonna believe you, are they?'

Tony looked down at his shoes for a moment. When again he raised his head, the sneer was back. 'Yeah, well,' he said, 'I don't have to explain myself to you, thank you.'

He wheeled and marched briskly towards the sergeants' mess. Paddy and Dave tilted their heads and looked at one another in that Paddy and Dave way. It was one of the things about the army. Again and again, you saw your mates making fools of themselves, and, having said your bit, there was bugger all else you could do but watch as they slithered down the primrose path.

That night, Tony slid the final few feet. It was

Ellie's evening off. He turned up in her porch with a bottle of wine. She greeted him in the most familiar and welcoming way of all. She simply opened the door, said 'Hi!' and walked back to the sitting-room, leaving Tony to make his own way in.

And it started again – the inconsequential statements, the elastic glances. 'Do you mind?' Tony asked as soon as he passed the threshold. 'I mean, I mean, if you're busy. . .' Then he realized that he was in, and said, 'Thanks.'

'I've had a terrible day. . .' Tony continued, 'but my report about Milburn. . . That's had an effect. . .'

She stood waiting for him in the darkened living room. 'You brought some wine,' she said.

'Yeah. Well, I thought. . .'

'Thanks.'

'You got some. . .? Well, of course you got some glasses. Sorry. . .'

And again she was in his arms, warm and smelling of apple-sheds and hay, and her lips were giving beneath his, her tongue tracing a flickering trail about his gums, her arms clasping him close.

'You need a shave,' she said in a small voice as she laid her cheek against his shoulder.

'Look. Ellie.' He looked up at the ceiling and tried to still the quavering of his voice. 'Look, I don't want to rock the boat. I can't help myself. I don't want. . .'

'Tony,' she said, 'You wouldn't have come here if you hadn't wanted this to happen.'

'I want you,' he said huskily.

'It's the same thing,' she whispered back. She laid her fingertips against his and led him through the room to a white door. She pushed it open. The room was softly lit by lamps on either side of the bed. There was another bottle of wine glistening at the right of the bed, and two glasses. Something clasped at Tony's Adam's apple. Ellie turned to him with a rustle of fabric. She said 'Tony. . .'

He breathed. 'Ellie. . .' She fell back on to the bed, and for a long time afterwards, those were the only words that they spoke.

Joy Wilton bore the large, heart-shaped cake into Donna's flat like a herald with a ceremonial key. 'There,' she said softly as she laid it on the coffee-table.

'What's that?' Donna winced.

'The cake you said you'd take, dear.'

'Cake? I never said anything about a cake!'

'You did, Donna,' she reproved. 'I asked if you'd take something. . .'

'Yeah, OK, but I was thinking a photo or a book or something. I can't sit all the way to

Auckland with a flamin' gateau on my knee!'

'Donna. . .?' Mrs Deeley poked her head around the jamb of the kitchen door.

'What d'ye want, Mam?'

'Oh, sorry. Didn't realize you had company. Sorry, Mrs Wilton. Donna, I was wondering if you could give us a hand with this recipe. . .'

'Recipe? Yeah, OK. Hold on.' Donna turned back to Joy, 'I mean, I'll be covered in icing and. . .'

'Right now, please, Donna. It's boiling over. . .'

'Oh, Gawd. What's boiling over? What are you *doing*, Mam? Hold it, Joy. . .'

Donna dragged her fluffy slippers as she walked to the kitchen. No sooner was she past the door frame than the door swung shut behind her.

'Sh!' her mother told her.

'What's goin' on, Mam?' Donna whispered, frowning.

'You carry that bloody cake or you forget your trip, my girl,' Mrs Deeley hissed. 'She's meant to be helping me out with Macaulay, remember? She asks you to carry a pig, you just tell her you love pigskin luggage, you hear?'

It was a subdued Donna who slouched back into the sitting-toom. 'I don't know,' she said pointedly. 'They get that confused at that age. No, but listen, Joy, it'll go stale, won't it?'

'Oh, no. No, it's an all-butter recipe with excellent keeping qualities,' Joy reassured her.

'It would be,' muttered Donna. 'Right. Yes. If I can get it in a box. . .'

She looked down with loathing at the object with its impeccable copperplate legend, *Tony, I love you, Joy.*

Tuesday dawned murky in Hong Kong. The sky was low and the colour of an aged bruise. Whilst their men were still in bed, the girls were up and giggling excitedly as they made their final preparations. Mrs Deeley was so terrified at the prospect of divorce which Donna had sketched that she was acting more like a madame than a mother. 'Now, pet, you've got your backless black?' she checked.

'Aye,' said Donna, 'but with the black courtshoes or the red slingbacks?'

'Well, if the row was as bad as you say, go for the slingbacks,' said Mrs Deeley firmly. 'This is no time for subtlety.'

Sheena was unconcerned about packing. She kept her eyes on the sky and asked, for the fifth time so far this morning, 'You're sure it's all right? I mean, they won't fly if it's rough, will they?'

'What do you want, Sheen?' Nancy asked. 'I mean, you've rung the weatherboard, the airline. . ... It'll be OK. Relax.'

'I can't!' Sheena protested.

'You know the statistics,' Nancy told her. 'You're a damned sight safer up there than you are crossing the street.'

'Yeah, but I'm in control on the street,' Sheena protested. 'Up there. . . It's unnatural.'

'We'll be with you,' Nancy smiled. She could see that Sheena was not to be consoled, and decided that briskness was called for. 'Right. Everyone got passports?'

'Yeah,' said Donna.

'You're sure. . .?' Sheena started.

'Passports?' Nancy interrupted.

'Oh, yeah, but listen. . .'

'Tickets?'

Donna waved the folder. 'Right here,' she said.

'Driver's licence?'

'Haven't got one,' said Sheena in a very small voice.

'Dunno where mine's gone,' Donna shrugged.

'Oh, well, I've got mine,' Nancy sighed. 'It's in my case.' She patted the grey Samsonite. She stood. 'Right, let's be going.'

'Here,' Donna frowned at Nancy's suitcase, 'Is that lockable? Can I put my heated rollers in it?'

Nancy's eyes rolled heavenward, but Mrs Deeley said, 'Oh, very wise, pet. Very wise.'

Five minutes later, Nancy contrived to herd the girls on to the landing. Donna kissed her mam and poked Macaulay's stomach with a finger. 'Tara, thunderguts,' she grinned.

And, as they clattered down the stairs, Sheena said, 'I mean, you hear about turbulence, electric storms and that. I mean, we're not talking about proper British aeroplanes here. . .'

They were on their way.

Tuesday dawned clear and bright in New Zealand. A feathery breeze lifted the hair off Dave Tucker's brow as he shovelled the rich red soil from the bottom of the trench. 'I don't know,' he whined, 'I joined the bloody army to fight for Her Majesty, not to do landscape bloody gardening.'

Vinny obviously caught the 'landscape' bit, but his spade crunched into the ground or one of the men grunted on the 'gardening'. 'I do a bit of painting,' he said, and flung a spadeful of soil. 'I used to do the scenery for the music and drama society back home.'

'Yeah?' Midnight heaved. 'Well, young Vincent, you are now about to appear in a live version of *South Pacific*.'

'Bloody live firing exercise,' droned Dave, 'bloody round robin, bloody trenches. . .'

His moaning was interrupted by a faceful of dirt dropped on his head. He spluttered and turned, lips already pulled back off his teeth, eyes glinting in anticipation of a fight. Milburn stood above him with a gap-toothed grin of triumph.

Dave snarled, 'Bastard!' He was out of that trench like a jack-in-the-box, his spade swinging.

Milburn stepped back from the flailing blade. He held his spade defensively across his chest. He chewed gum noisily. 'Yeah, well, I've had two days of no birds and booze thanks to you,' he growled.

'Oy!' Tony Wilton's voice rang as he marched briskly over to the two men. 'Milburn! It wasn't Tucker who informed on you. It was me.' He moved between the two men and stood with his face just inches from the New Zealander's, his jaw thrust forward. 'So. . .?' he invited.

'Yeah, well. . .' Milburn's eyes shifted to right and left. 'If you don't tidy up your act. . .'

'Yeah?' Tony smiled, 'Come on, then. . .?'

'Good morning, gentlemen!' Kieran Voce had a gift for this sort of timing. His voice was calm – casual, even – but both men snapped to attention. There was a chorus of 'sirs' from the trench. Kieran returned the salute. 'Ah, Sergeant. If you please,' he said to Tony, then, 'Carry on, guys.'

Tony Wilton fell in at Kieran's left side. Kieran led him out of earshot of the others. He stared straight ahead as he spoke. 'Words to the wise, Sergeant. . .'

Tony gulped. 'Sir?'

'Your private life's your own, of course. . .'

'Yes, I know, Sir.'

'. . .provided, of course, that it remains private. But if your behaviour begins to undermine your authority as a senior NCO. . .'

'Sir, it's not. . .' began Tony, but the words would not come.

'. . .then that is an entirely different kettle of fish,' continued Kieran smoothly. Now he looked at Tony for the first time. 'You're in the frame for colour sergeant, aren't you?'

'Yes, Sir.' Tony was sulky.

'Well, we want NCOs who reflect a mature authority, men in whom soldiers – and their families – can place their trust and respect.'

'Yes, Sir,' Tony rasped. He could not meet Kieran's gaze.

Kieran drew himself up and turned back to a perusal of the scenery. He punched his palm. 'Right. Well. Hope I've said enough, Sergeant.'

'Yes. Thank you, Sir.'

'Right.' Kieran glanced at his watch. 'Better be getting the men mustered for this exercise, then. Bit of a needle-match, by the look of things.'

'Yes, Sir.'

'Carry on, Sergeant.'

Tony Wilton's cheeks burned as he trotted back to the trench and fired off orders. He found refuge in action. His anger and embarrassment, so far from distracting him, forced him to ever greater commitment and ferocity. He supervised the preparation of camo – the mud-streaks to diminish reflections from faces and hands, the stuffing of packs, belts and helmets with the bone-coloured scrub which covered the hills. No detail was too small. Here, for Tony, was certainty.

By the time Kieran and Osbourne returned for the obligatory pep talk before the off, Tony was satisfied that his men, at least, were properly equipped and suitably fired-up for the exercise.

'Gentlemen,' Kieran told them all, 'You are now at the start-point for the round robin exercise. You know the drill. The sheets provided give the grid references of all the stands and the order in which you must appear at them. The stands are approximately two miles apart, and we've set up a fair mixture of challenges for you. You'll be tested not only on your fitness and map reading but also on field craft, first aid, chemical reaction drills and a whole lot more besides. This is a competition, lads. Remember, think tactically at all times and expect the unexpected. You may regret it if you don't. Best endeavours from all concerned, please. Colonel?'

Osbourne had conventional words to offer – and a good, if superfluous bit of advice. 'Good luck,' he said, 'May the best man win. Don't get lost.' He turned to Tony. 'Sergeant,' he said with a nod.

Tony hooked his arm and held his watch at eye level. He raised his other arm as though he were holding the starter's flag. The secondhand jerked round. . .

'First section. . .' Tony yelled, 'Ready to move out! And. . . go!'

And, with whoops and yells, Paddy Garvey's section went.

'Ohhh,' Sheena groaned as the girls rode down the escalator. 'Oh, God. That was horrible.'

'It weren't that bad, was it, Nance?' Donna turned to call back over Sheena's shoulder.

'Nice smooth flight.' Nancy shrugged. 'You make yourself ill by worrying, Sheena. You should have taken some of Donna's mam's tranquillizers. I did tell you.'

'Yeah, but I'd rather be awake when I die.'

'Well, I told you,' Donna stopped at the bottom of the escalator. 'If you'd put bits of brown paper in your bra, you'd have had no problem.'

'Anyhow, we're here now,' Nancy drew abreast of the other two as they collected a trolley and headed for the luggage carousel. 'All we have to do's pick up the luggage, rent a car and we're away. Should be here by now. . .' she eyed the suitcases circling. 'Donna, that's yours, isn't it?'

'Yeah.' Donna laid the cakebox down on the edge of the carousel, and, with a weightlifter's roar, heaved the nylon holdall on to the trolley.

It was another five minutes before Nancy voiced her frustration. 'Come on!' she said. 'We've been twenty minutes in the bog. What are they doing?'

Nancy caught sight of a red-headed man who had been in the row ahead of them during the flight. He was now at the queue for the Bureau de Change. She scampered over to him. The other girls watched as she talked, nodded, pointed and smiled. He shrugged and returned the smile.

Nancy spotted a woman in the airline's uniform. The woman had a profile like a headsman's axe with a cottage-loaf on top. Nancy was only one of several travellers who gathered about her, gabbling questions. The woman looked and spoke as if she were a schoolma'am and the passengers naughty brats. More aggrieved passengers joined the convention. The axe-headed woman led them over to a desk and instructed them to queue. Nancy was third from the front. The woman asked each of the passengers questions. She wrote as Nancy answered. Donna frowned as she watched the whole business.

'They can't have,' she muttered. 'Dear God, please, no. . .'

'I've still got bits of sick stuck up the back of me nose,' said Sheena.

'Oh, no. Tell me it's not true. . .' Donna shifted from foot to foot as though desperate for a pee as Nancy walked back towards them, her mouth set in a rigid dash.

'Bangkok,' she announced. She flung herself down in a chair.

'You what?' Donna wailed. '*Bangkok*?'

'Yeah, brilliant, isn't it? Not to Auckland. Oh, no. Not even to London. How do they do it? Bloody Bangkok.'

'What?' Sheena blinked. 'What about Bangkok?'

'Your case and mine,' Nancy explained wearily, 'are the lucky winners of an unscheduled trip to beautiful, exotic Bangkok. Good start, eh?'

'But – what are we going to do?' Sheena asked.

'Oh, it's not that bad,' Donna held up halting hands. 'Let's calm down, OK? You can borrow things of mine. . .' Her mature, controlled tone and expression suddenly dissolved. 'Eee!' she shrieked like chalk, 'Hang on! Me heated rollers are in your case!'

'Right.' Nancy was languid. 'And so is my driver's licence.'

'So how'd we get to Wyoulou?' Sheena's head jerked this way and that as though a solution might be lurking in a corner.

'Woah. Stop. Steady.' Nancy stood. 'Stop. Think. The British Army never panics.'

'Well, I bloody do!' Donna's slow dance had become a frantic tarantella. Her hand rose to her hair. 'I mean, you can't maintain a style like this with spit and a packet of kirby-grips!'

Nancy came to a decision. 'Look, if we all pool our money, we should be able to afford a train-ticket each.'

'Pool our money?' Donna was suspicious.

'Yup. Look, we're all in this together, Donna. And some of us have a little more than others.'

'Meaning me, I suppose.' Donna bit off the words and spat them out in foul-tasting chunks. 'Oh, yes, I saw you clocking me mam giving me some extra. Well, listen to me, Nancy Garvey. It's not my cases that've gone walkabout, is it? And I'm not here for the good of my health. I'm here to save my marriage. I might have to spend that cash on – I dunno – a candlelit dinner, some perfume, something. . .' She fell suddenly silent, her mouth still open wide. She stared.

Nancy hadn't noticed. 'Look, Donna, if you want to see Dave at all today, let alone candlelit bloody dinners, you're going to have to shut up and cough up and have done. We've got two hundred miles to cover.'

Donna closed her mouth. She tried to speak a couple of times, but all that came out was a series of strange little noises that might have been made by an unhappy puppy. She licked her lips and tried again. 'I can't. . .' she blurted at last. 'The money's in the box with me rollers!'

Sheena and Nancy exchanged glances. Their shoulders sank. Nancy slumped back into the chair. 'Oh, that's great,' she said. 'That's altogether bloody great.'

Two hundred miles away, unbeknownst to them, their men were practising survival and wayfinding techniques. That, however, was a game. For the girls, it was the real thing.

Paddy Garvey flung himself down beneath the low ridge. He heard rather than saw his men puffing and rattling as they too fell into the cover. He looked around him. All present and correct. He had had them replace the scrub camo with foliage before they entered this wood. He unfolded the sheet of paper in his left hand. He nodded.

'OK, lads,' he whispered, 'We're making good time. Next stand should be just over there through those trees. All set? Let's go.'

They walked on, then, keeping low and weaving through the sporadic cover of the forest, each man covering both flanks and his rear as he went. Paddy saw Dave down at his right, alert, totally into it, and thought, 'If it weren't for his bloody temperament, he'd be the best natural soldier of us all.' He saw Vinny at his left and again felt that Vinny would need watching and restraint. He just loved it all so much – he loved just about everything so much – that he overran himself, tripped on his own feet in his keenness. If only you could transplant a little of Vinny's verve into Dave, a little of Dave's sourness and scepticism into Vinny. . .

Gunfire rattled. Red and yellow Very flares described graceful parabolas against the trees and lay hissing and pumping thick smoke which rapidly filled the glade.

'Gas!' Paddy shrieked, 'Gas! Gas! Gas!'

He closed his eyes tight and fumbled for his respirator. He had been in a genuine gas-attack in the Gulf, and reckoned that, if he heard those words when asleep at the age of ninety, he could still perform the drill to perfection. Only when he had the gasmask securely on did he look around to check on his platoon.

Dave was all right. He had been in the same unit as Paddy back there in Kuwait. For him too, it was a matter of terrified reflex. For Vinny, it was a matter of recent training. Midnight, however, had never known gas in earnest, and his training was long forgotten. Oh, he got the respirator to his muzzle, but the quick clunk-click which should have been automatic was cumbersome and slow. 'Oh, shit! Oh, shit!' he howled as the smoke filled his eyes and lungs, and Paddy was transported back to the desert, where he had heard the same frantic screaming from Fusilier Doran as he sank to his knees and, bare minutes later, wheezing and honking, violently convulsed and died.

Captain Voce emerged from behind the trees. 'OK, OK. Not bad, not bad,' he called. 'Rawlings, unfortunately, was a goner from the word go. Received alert, kept his eyes open, made a complete pig's ear of respirator drill. That's a five minute penalty.'

Midnight, eyes streaming, removed his helmet and thumped it down on to the leafy ground. 'Shit!' he sang. 'Oh, shit!'

'Right,' said Kieran, 'the chemical situation is now zero. Your team is ten points down. Change en route.' He looked down at his watch. 'And. . . Go!'

Chapter 6

They had persuaded the red-headed man, who turned out to be a British stockbroker, to give them a lift out on to the main road. He had said, 'Damn bad luck. Shame I'm headed in the wrong direction. Like to do my bit for the boys in blue – sterling body of men, England's finest, where would we be without them, eh? Fancied an army career myself, but my mother wouldn't hear of it – no, like to help, but there you are. Business, I'm afraid. Needs must when the devil drives.' He had left them at a roundabout with strict instructions that they should not accept lifts from strange men. The girls had looked at one another seriously. They had nodded. Only when he had driven out of sight had they let the laughter burst from them.

'Boys in blue' had kept them happy for the first ten minutes or so. After twenty minutes standing there with their thumbs stuck out whilst cars swept by with a tinfoil sizzle, they could no longer see what was so funny about it.

'Bloody typical, isn't it?' Donna had sighed. 'When I think of the number of times, I've told kerb-crawlers to piss off, and now when you want a lift... Where are all the red-blooded males in this country?'

'Even the creeps,' Nancy had agreed.

At length, a long-haired student in a jeep had taken them as far as Hamilton. Donna had been reluctant to climb into an open-topped vehicle. Her coiffure, she pointed out, would be considerably altered by such an experience, and the means to make good the damage were in Thailand. Sheena had climbed up and firmly said, 'Bugger your kwuffer, Donna. Get up here.'

The young man had driven fast.

Donna had been quite forcefully reminded of Blackie, her cat when she was a child. Blackie had climbed into the tumbledrier one day, and someone had casually shut the door. Blackie had emerged stiff as a board with his mouth fossilized in a perpetual snarl and his usually sleek fur bouffant. This, she thought as she rocked from side to side at a corner or lurched backward and forward as the driver braked, was what Blackie must have felt like. The only difference was that Blackie had at least had the comfort of warmth, whereas Donna was blasted by cold air which made her eyes weep black tears and seemed to wriggle into every part of her.

Conversation was impossible, but that did not stop the driver from essaying it. He repeatedly shouted something which was blown away on the wind, and Nancy or Sheena would shout back, 'What?' or 'Yes!' and grin. Donna neither spoke nor grinned. With one hand she clutched the bloody cake on her lap, with the other, she held her hair, feeling hank after hank tugged from its confines. She needed more hands, to ward off the side of the jeep which kept hitting at her lower ribs, and to pick specks from her eyes, but she couldn't find them.

It was funny, the way things went. Sheena had been groaning when they had disembarked from the aeroplane. Now she was positively perky, and kept closing her eyes and shaking her head in the wind as though she enjoyed it, and it was Donna who released a foghorn moan as at last she slid from the jeep and staggered on the verge.

She was altogether too ill to do anything but sit on the grass while Sheena and Nancy strutted their stuff in the hope of enticing a lift. Of course, sod's law, which seemed to be operating with peculiar consistency today, dictated that, for all their efforts, they were picked up not by a hunk in a Ferrari but a haggard old woman in a farmtruck. The rear of the truck was full of sheep, so the girls had to squeeze into the cab, suitcase, cake and all.

'So,' said the woman. She shoved the gearstick and the engine made a noise like a constipated donkey before shuddering into movement. 'So, where are you from, then?'

'Hong Kong,' said Nancy. 'Well, Britain, really, but we're living in Hong Kong.'

'Poms, eh?' The woman exhibited some teeth that you would expect to see exhibited in an archaeological museum. 'And where are you going today, then?'

'Wyoulou,' Nancy told her.

'Oh, yes?' The woman looked at Donna's micro-skirt. 'Give the boys a cheap thrill, eh? I'd've thought you'd make enough money to travel in style.'

'What?' Sheena frowned.

'I mean, Hong Kong's a good pitch, isn't it? All those soldiers, bankers, I dunno. Then a trip like this. Wyoulou. Hundreds of guys down there, right? Should be coining it.'

The girls looked at one another. For a moment, Sheena was affronted. She said, 'You've got it all wrong.' Then she saw the twinkle in the other girls' eyes.

'Nah,' the woman chided. 'Come on. I saw you on the roadside, flashing all you got. Don't get me wrong. I got no objection. Girl's got to make a living.'

'No, no,' said Nancy, 'We're not going for the sex.'

'Oh, no?' the woman harrumphed.

'No, we're setting up a peace camp by the barricades.'

The woman said, 'Hm,' and left it at that.

They were out in the open again, and their camo was once more the creamy grass of the hills. They were running in waves. Dave and his lads would go down and give covering fire whilst Paddy's group moved forward, then it was the forward party's turn to cover the others. Their destination was a hollow in the hillside. Paddy had selected it because of the boulders there.

Yes. Not a bad choice, he thought, as he flung himself on to the grass behind the largest and flattest of the stones. The valley floor behind them was wide open. No one could attack unseen from that direction, and the hollow afforded cover on either side. The only danger came from above, and at least, for now, the boulders offered partial protection. But it was up there that they must go. He scanned the hillside. . .

There. A watercourse, perhaps eighty yards away at its nearest point. . .

All about him, panting men were thudding to the ground. Dave Tucker, eyes hungrily swivelling, whispered, 'Any ideas where we are?'

'Yeah,' said Paddy, with more certainty than he felt.

'Go for the watercourse?' asked Dave.

'Yeah.' Paddy nodded.

'Can I take point, corp?' Vinny piped up, keen as ever. And, without waiting for a yes or no, he was up and breaking cover. Dave threw himself at him, brought him down, but already the guns above them were rattling.

'Ambush, lads!' Paddy barked. 'Take cover! Come on! Move!'

Even as he spoke, his section's guns started to stutter, and Paddy was pulling out the model grenade, gauging the exact position of the guns. He lobbed it. At almost the same moment, Dave, who had scrabbled behind the boulder, sent another grenade spinning in the same direction.

The guns fell silent.

Paddy exhaled with a noise like a horse. He wiped his mouth on his sleeve. He nodded to Dave.

'Right,' said the New Zealander who strode down the hill towards them. 'Nine out of ten for response to ambush, nil for navigation. This is the wrong stand at the wrong time.'

'Shit!' said Paddy.

'Bowles is a designated casualty,' the Kiwi continued. 'He'll have to be carried.'

'You wazzock!' Dave told Vinny.

Vinny looked as though he just might cry.

*

84

The girls were out in wild country now. The sun was already well on its downward path. It was getting colder. They still had forty miles to go. They had been well-pleased when this strange, wild-eyed moustachioed guy had pulled over to pick them up. Nice comfortable motor, heater purring, stereo twanging. He was headed for a place within ten miles of the base, and Donna was quietly confident that she could, with time, persuade him to make the diversion.

That was until he spoke.

'You look like modern sort of girls,' he said, and his cobwebbed eyes shifted to Sheena's thighs. 'Er. . . You wear stockings or pantihose?'

'I beg your pardon?' Donna twanged.

'No, sorry,' the man nodded. 'Just interested, you know. . . I mean, me, I wear pantihose.'

There was a moment of stunned silence, then Sheena's gaze moved down to the man's trouser-cuffs. The feet that worked the clutch and accelerator were sheathed in sheer white glistening tights and shod in high-heeled black patent courts.

Sheena shrieked.

'Oh, right. That's it!' Donna snapped.

'Stop the car!' Nancy ordered in her best parade-ground tones.

'Oh, dear.' The man braked hard. 'Oh, dear,' he fussed, 'I'm just so dreadfully embarrassed.'

The girls jumped out of there as fast as they could. They slammed the doors. Nancy went round the back to pull down the case and the cake. Donna gave the driver the benefit of her experience. 'You wanna be careful with tights on underneath them nylon slacks,' she shouted, 'You'll end up with crotch rot.'

'This country's full of nutters.' Sheena shook her head sadly as the car pulled away.

'No,' Nancy sighed. 'It's not New Zealand. It's hitching. Come on, girls. Onward and upward.'

'I'm bloody starving,' said Donna as she fell in behind the other two. 'Do you think this qualifies as a major disaster?'

'Pretty major, yes,' Sheena turned. 'Why?' She caught the direction of Donna's glance. 'No, Donna. No, no, no.' She reached back and snatched the cakebox. 'Don't even think about it.'

Donna scowled.

The girls trudged on.

Paddy had got his bearings now. The section was back on course and well ahead of the clock. Midnight and Vinny, under the rules of the competition, had miraculously recovered and rejoined the unit.

Paddy knew what this next stand entailed from two hundred yards off. The 'wounded' on the stretchers might win no Oscars, but what they lacked in subtlety, they more than made up for in volume. They moaned and gargled and screamed and struggled whilst the previous section ministered to them under Tony Wilton's eye.

Paddy reckoned that they could never have been there. Not for real.

'All right, Florence,' he said to Dave. 'You did the course. Let's see what they taught you at that medic school.'

'Yeah,' Dave grinned. 'Great.'

'You'd better be, if we're going to win this war.'

'Right!' Tony Wilton yelled. He was once more looking at his watch. 'And. . . Time's up! Fall in, two ranks, here! Now! Behind me!'

The soldiers abandoned their patients and moved at the double to form ranks.

'Move it move it move it!' Tony chivvied. 'Right, which one of you stupid bastards has just administered morphine to the fellow with his head blown open?'

There was a pause, then a soldier stepped forward. 'Sarge,' he said quietly.

'Right, lose ten points, wait five minutes, get out of my sight!'

'Yes,' whispered Vinny gleefully.

'Great,' said Dave.

'Let's keep cool,' Paddy soothed.

Tony turned to Paddy. 'Corporal Garvey,' he snapped, 'Six wounded, fifteen minutes, do your best work.'

Paddy entered the compound at the trot. The wounded resumed their groaning. Dave took in the scene and fired out orders. 'Vinny, mouth to mouth over on the right. Paddy, burns case. Midnight. . .' he tossed over the pack, 'if you give morphine, remember your drill.'

Paddy watched his friend with admiration. There was no one that he'd rather have with him in war. It was peace that Dave wasn't so good at.

'They'll find our remains by the roadside,' Donna intoned like a drunkard. She dragged her feet but walked on because the road was moving back- ward, and she'd fall over if she didn't. 'Just bones and luggage. . . and three poxy wedding rings.'

'Yeah, well, faint heart never won fair soldier, Donna.' Nancy, thought Donna, would make a very good kindergarten teacher. It was all very well for her. She was in training.

Donna tottered on through the dusk. Their last lift – a seven mile ride – had been on a trailer pulled by a poxy tractor, for God's sake. There were still eighteen miles to go. 'And I could eat a scabby dog. I still think we should eat that cake, only Postman Pat here won't take her mitts off it.'

'No, Donna,' said Sheena. 'You can't betray someone's trust like that. Anyway – look!'

They were rounding a corner, and Sheena, with all the theatricality of a conjuror, was indicating a roadhouse. The sun was sinking behind its roof, but you could still see ROADHOUSE writ in red above the door.

'Oh, Toto,' droned Donna. 'Whoopee. The Emerald City,' But it was noticeable that she picked up her feet and doubled her walking pace as they made their way across the road and through the door. She grabbed the nearest chair and slumped down in it. She kicked off her shoes.

Nancy looked around. It was one of those cafeteria affairs where you pushed your tray along the metallic counter, lifted flaps to pull cold food from plastic boxes, then came to the steaming stainless-steel containers, changed your mind and took all the cold stuff back. A few men sat rumbling quietly at formica-topped tables about the walls. 'So, what's everyone having?' she asked.

'Ooh, thirty-seven cups of tea and a burger – a big one, all the trimmings – and chips,' said Donna. 'And that's for starters.'

'Right. You, Sheen?'

'Sounds good to me,' Sheena smiled. 'I'll give you a hand.'

The two girls left Donna to massage her feet.

They placed the order for burgers with an attractive, dark-haired woman and returned to the table with tea and orange-juice. 'Oooh,' Nancy creaked as she sat. 'Can't we just stop here?'

Donna spluttered on her tea. 'Are you on glue or what?'

'Yeah, well. . .' Nancy's lips twitched. 'It's all right for some. I mean, you guys, one quick surprise, surprise, a slightly longer snog and you're right back where you want to be. I tell you, the closer I get to Paddy, the more I worry about how he's going to take this. I dread it.'

'So what happened to "he'll be so chuffed"?' asked Donna.

'Yeah, in theory, sure, he's a newish man, but it's all theory, isn't it? Come down to it, they're all cavemen at heart.'

'Come down to it, that's how we want it,' Donna agreed.

'You may,' mused Nancy, 'and yes, OK, in some ways. . .'

'I don't,' said Sheena, 'and my Vinny's not a caveman.'

'Do you girls want gherkins on these?' called the woman at the counter.

Sheena had to turn to say 'Yes.' She was therefore spared the sight of Donna silently and scornfully miming 'My Vinny's not a caveman' with a Shirley Temple expression.

She also missed the sight of a man entering the room with a gun in his hands.

Nancy missed it too. Donna was now engaged in giving the glad eye to a man at a corner table. Nancy said, 'Oh, for God's sake, woman, give over, will you?'

'What?' Donna hunched down, conspiratorial, 'and miss the chance of a lift to the love of my life? No way.'

The waitress emerged carrying three piled-high plates. She said, 'Here you are, girls...'

It was at that moment that the man with the gun drew adjacent to Nancy. Her chair toppled. She was up, screaming, 'Look out!' She grabbed the gun barrel in one hand, the man's arm in the other, and she propelled him with startling force against the counter. The air was spiked with yelps. Nancy grasped the man's hair now and, kicking the backs of his knees to throw him off balance, flung him hard over a vacant table. The man, not without reason, looked startled as he slithered back on to the floor. His head hit the tiles with a crack. A second later, the gun boomed.

There was more yelping. The waitress squealed. The plates smashed to the floor. Shot pattered about the room. Plaster then pattered on the floor above the ringing of the echo, the buzzing of the windows. Nancy closed in again.

She stamped on the man's wrist and ground her heel in hard. His mouth opened in a silent scream. His fingers opened. Nancy reached down for the gun. She kicked the man in the gut, just to keep him down, as she straightened. He gasped, rolled over on to his side, clasped his belly and writhed.

'What the bleedin' hell's going on in here?' The voice from the doorway sang in the walls.

Donna and Sheena emerged from beneath the table. They saw a dark, curly-haired, muscular man in an open-necked shirt. Donna said, 'Ooh, that'll do me. Here, Modesty Blaise!' she called to Nancy, 'You've got tomato sauce all over you.'

Nancy was tough, but she looked down at her clothes and said, 'Oh, bloody hell! No?'

She might shed blood, but she did like to keep it off her outfit.

Chapter 7

The girls had had a tough day. Their men had had a stroll.

God, just look at them, making much of their aches and pains, heaving breath as they ran to the top of the river-bank. Donna could not have mustered so much as a cheer at this moment, but, when Paddy's section ran up to the Kiwi sergeant to hear, 'OK, this section here through first,' which meant they were in the lead, Paddy, Dave, Vinny and Co. gave a whoop fit to raise the rafters.

So they would be first on the final stage – the death-slide across the river and the run for home. They were within an ace of victory.

The New Zealanders who had started before them stood sourly grimacing as, one by one, the Poms grasped the rope slung through the steel figure-of-eight and swung across the river. Dave Tucker was the last to go. He winked at Milburn. 'You did real good, Lance Corporal,' he called, 'Well, done!'

Milburn glared. Dave said, 'Wheee!' and kicked off.

On the other bank, Dave spent a short while dealing with the apparatus. He trotted up to join the rest of his section on the grass. Home was not far away.

'On the double,' Paddy ordered, 'Come on, lads! We've got this one! Go!'

The section moved forward. Dave fell in beside Paddy.

'They can still catch up with us, mate,' Paddy called as he ran.

'Mmm, they could. . .' Dave grinned, 'but I don't think they will.'

Paddy knew him too well, knew that sly, amused glint in his eye. 'All right,' he said. 'Come on. Why not?'

'Oh, I just pinched the rope!' Dave waved it from the deathslide above his head.

Paddy laughed. Under the eyes of the disgusted Kiwis on the other side of the river, Dave Tucker swung the precious rope and broke into raucous song. 'The hills are alive with the sound of music. . .!'

Vinny hooted and skipped. He had mates. It felt great.

By the time the policeman had taken statements, commended Nancy for her courage and driven the unfortunate guntoter away, it was half past eight. By the time Alex, the owner of the road-

94

house, and her brother Don, the hunk who had taken the problem and the gun over from Nancy, had said their apologies and expressed their gratitude and made it up to the girls with a slap-up meal, it was half-past ten. Sheena and Donna sat tired, relaxed and replete as Nancy went upstairs with Donna's case to change.

'So he's done this before, has he?' said Donna.

'Yeah,' Alex smiled. 'Somehow, I don't think he'll do it again!'

'Serve the pranny right,' said Don. 'I've warned him. I mean, there's no harm in him, but he just thinks it's kind of cool, you know? Walk in from the fields with a gun. . .'

'A loaded gun!' said Sheena.

'Yeah, well that was sheer bloody stupid,' Don growled. 'He's barred for life, I can tell you. And he'll lose his permit.'

'Yeah, Sam says he'll do time for it,' said Alex, 'but the best bit is mister macho man with his big phallic symbol getting the shit kicked out of him by a girl like Nancy – and a Pom, too! Look, I'll get her clothes washed tonight, send them over tomorrow, OK?'

'Thanks,' said Sheena. She turned as she heard the clatter of Nancy's feet on the staircase. Two very long stockinged legs emerged first, then a strip of black fabric, then a bodice that hugged like oil. 'Way hey!' Sheena called. Donna wolf-whistled. Alex cheered. Don said appreciatively, 'Atta girl. Show us what you're made of.'

The head which emerged atop this vision was looking stern and embarrassed. 'Yeah, well, I'm sorry I took so long,' Nancy said. 'I mistook Donna's skirt for a headband.'

'All set, then?' Don stood.

'Yup,' said Sheena, Donna and Nancy as one. The long day's journey was almost done.

'So how long'll it take us to Wyoulou?' asked Donna as they made for the door.

'Less than an hour with my foot down.' Don held open the door to allow them to pass through. 'And if they're soldiers, I reckon I know where to find them. . .'

The Hot Lava was hot tonight. The joint was thumping. The Kiwis might sit staring into their drinks, but the Brits were in the mood to celebrate, and had no intention of doing so with reserve or subtlety. Beer glass in hand, Dave stood on a table beneath a strand of smoke to lead a chorus of that universal anthem, '*Earwig O*'. Vinny pogoed like a punk as he sang, a broad grin all over his face, his cheeks glowing like pippins. Sweat glistened on Midnight's beaming face. Paddy's cheeks were flushed and his eyes bright.

The Earwig song made way for the equally inevitable chant of *We Are the Champions*.

'Yeah, by three lousy points!' shouted Milburn.

'Three hard-earned, precious, lovely points more than you lot!' Dave retorted. 'Face it, man, we stuffed you!'

Milburn glared, then shrugged. A suspicion of a smile even tugged at his lips.

'Now listen up, ladies!' called Tony Wilton in his best town-crier style. He marched to the centre of the floor. 'Bit of hush, if you please. Sergeant Wilton with a very, very important speech to make!'

Whistles and catcalls greeted this announcement. They subsided. Tony continued, 'Right, now here is the good news. Commanding officers in their wisdom and munificence have donated a crate of ale. . .'

Paddy was at the forefront of the cheering at this news.

'. . .but take it easy. Don't want everyone getting legless, because Company Sergeant Major has called for a curfew!'

Predictably, this caused booing. Tony grinned. 'Everybody in the barracks by midnight, otherwise you get your bits chopped off. I thank you!' he bowed and marched swiftly back to the bar. Such eyes as followed him, which included Paddy's, saw Ellie lean across the bar to kiss him fill on the lips, saw Tony nervously glance about him, mutter a few words of reproof, saw Ellie, plainly pissed off, walk off in dudgeon.

Tony called after her, and would have pursued, but Paddy got in his way. 'Hi, Tone,' he said, 'Having fun?'

'Yeah.' Tony's grin came on and off like a flashlight. His eyes still followed Ellie.

'So, a good result, eh?'

'Yeah. Yeah, very good.'

'It's improved relations with the Kiwis, levelled things up,' Paddy said. 'They're not bad sorts.'

'No.'

'Amazing really, to think that, in a couple of weeks from now, we'll be on the other side of the world, never see them again. Wouldn't like to see any damage done, something as unimportant as that. . .'

That got through. That sneer curled Tony's lip again. 'You trying to say something, are you, Corporal Garvey?'

'Me? Oh, no, Sergeant.' Paddy was all innocence. 'You know me. And I know you, Tone, know that you're not so dumb as to muck everything up for the sake of a bit of skirt.'

Tony's eyes were marbles. 'You don't know shit,' he spat. 'When I need a bloody agony aunt, I'll call Claire Rayner, thanks. 'Ere, Ellie!'

Paddy pursed his lips and raised an eyebrow. He nodded. He strolled back to Dave. 'Our Tone's got it bad,' he sighed.

'That's the trouble with being the sort that doesn't play away.' Dave swigged from a bottle. He gasped and belched. 'I mean, you and me, my old mucker, we may have our little extra-curriculars, but we keep 'em in their place. Tony has a bit on the side, it's Romeo and Juliet revisited. Ah, well. Nothing we can do. Eat, drink and be merry, eh?'

'For tomorrow we die?' Paddy reflected. 'Yeah. You might have a point there.'

They were wreathed in smoke and steam when they lurched from the bar into the cold night air. Tony shepherded them out, 'On your way, soldiers. Do your talking while you're walking. Er. . . Listen, I'm busting for the loo. Be out in two minutes. Catch you up, right?'

'Yeah, right, Tone.' Paddy caught his eye. 'You have a nice leak.'

Tony scowled and ducked back into the club. His footfalls ran on ahead of him and pattered up the stairs. Ellie was up there at the bar. Her fist burrowed into a pint glass. She studiously did not look up as Tony leaped up the steps, three at a time.

'Ellie,' said Tony. The word echoed. He looked

about him, gulped and tried it again, quieter this time. 'Listen, Ellie. Look, I'm sorry.'

She laid down the glass and walked close to him. 'Everyone knows about us, Tony,' she said. 'Yeah. . . Sorry. . .'

And again he was drawn into the darkness of her. Her plush lips were yielding beneath his and their tongues intertwining, and he felt himself trembling with desire. He clasped her buttocks and pulled her up from the ground. 'God, Ellie,' he breathed, 'I need you. . .'

She placed a finger against his lips, took his hand and, without a word, led him through the gap in the bar to a door at the back. 'I've only got a few minutes,' Tony whispered, then wondered why he was whispering.

She turned and reached past him to push the office door shut. She linked her fingers at the back of his neck. 'So let's not waste a second,' she said.

The soldiers were still milling around the door-way when the car drew up and screeched to a halt. Paddy did a perfect Disney double take. He saw Nancy's grinning face, but it couldn't be Nancy, so he turned away. Then he frowned, realized that it *was* Nancy and said 'Jesus!'

Dave was off the mark a deal faster, but then Donna showed a great deal of leg as she stepped from the car, and the uncharitable might suggest that Dave always moved fast towards a great deal of leg, and the subsequent discovery that it was his wife's merely came as a surprise. A pleasant surprise, of course.

As for Vinny, he saw his Sheena and stood stock still, transfixed and beaming. Sheena was the first, amidst whoops from all around, to run into her man's arms. She said, 'Hiya' as though they had parted at breakfast that morning. He just said, 'Sheen. . .,' and hugged her as though to crush her ribs.

Donna engulfed Dave. She wanted there to be no doubt but that he was forgiven. After the first long kiss, she murmured, 'Happy anniversary, pet.'

'Oh, shit,' Dave shook the beery stupor from his head. 'Sorry, love. I forgot.'

'It doesn't matter. I love you.' Again she opted for means of expression more telling than language.

Dave came up for air and looked over at the car. 'Did you bring Macaulay with you?' he asked. Again the uncharitable might have detected a note of apprehension in his voice, and suggested that he was very much hoping that the answer would be in the negative.

'Did not!' Donna remonstrated. 'Come here, you.'

No octopus had as many limbs as Donna seemed to have when she was in affectionate mode.

Paddy's and Nancy's reunion was more decorous, more restrained, perhaps, but no less affectionate. She said, 'Hiya, love,' and he managed, 'Mrs Garvey' before kissing her.

What with Tony inside, the 'Make Love Not War' brigade would have smiled upon the King's Fusiliers tonight.

Sweetness and light, alas, are ephemeral. The first tang of sourness, the first fleecy cloud, came when Paddy softly asked, 'So what brings you here, love?'

'I had to talk to you,' Nancy kissed him again. 'I've been offered a place on a sergeant's course. Ten weeks back in the UK. I had to see you before I accepted.'

Paddy winced. 'D'ye want to accept?'

'Yes, Paddy. I do. I really do.'

Paddy raised his right hand to his brow. He closed his eyes to think. He knew that he had reasons to object. He just couldn't think at the moment what they were. He rolled his eyes towards the stars. He shook his head. He came up with the ultimate argument for conservatism: fear of change. 'Come on, Nance, we've got so much going for us. Everything's going fine. Why d'you want to go and spoil it? Why rock the boat?'

'I don't want to spoil it, Paddy,' she spoke quietly.

'Yeah, but that's what it means, isn't it? Different ranks, separate postings. . .'

'Where's Tony?' called Donna.

'Yeah, Tony? We've got a present for you!' Sheena piped up.

Nancy stepped back. She said, 'Look, we'll discuss this later, OK?' then, louder, 'Yeah, where's Tony hiding?'

'Don't think he's come out yet, has he Paddy?'

'I don't give a shit, mate.' Paddy was clasping the bridge on his nose between forefinger and thumb.

Nancy cast a quick glance at him. 'Let's go and find him,' she said.

The girls clattered across the road and pushed open the door of the Hot Lava. Donna, proudly bearing the hitherto hated cake, looked around and called 'Tone?'

'Tony!'

A New Zealand soldier called softly after them. 'Oy, girls! I think he's giving someone a hand at the back of the bar.'

'Ta, cheers,' said Nancy.

The New Zealander sank back into the shadows outside with a small smile.

Milburn had scored his small revenge.

The girls climbed the steps to the level of the bar. Something about the nature of their mission and the haunted hush of the place made them giggle nervously. 'There,' said Donna. She pointed at the door.

They found the flap in the bar. Nancy said, 'Sh!' Sheena released a little rivulet giggle. At the door, Nancy counted in a whisper. 'One, two, *three*!' She pushed open the door.

Nancy made a noise like a fanfare.

Donna said 'Tony!'

Sheena laughed.

All three fell very suddenly silent.

Tony's jaw dropped. He said, 'Er. . .'

The girl beneath him was naked to the waist, but she made no move to cover her breasts. She lay there watching the women in the doorway with a dull expression as though she had been in that position since Tutankhamun was laid to rest, as though they, not she, had been the objects of curiosity.

Donna was more than a match for a bloody reclining Easter Island statue. She swept aside the dark woman's bra. She said, 'Don't mind us. We've brought a present for you. . .'

She laid the cake on the desk and stood back. 'From your wife,' she snapped. 'Good night.'

Then the British women were gone. Tony could do what he wished.

But at that moment, it didn't seem so appealing any more.

Then Ellie's hand moved against him. He looked down on her glistening lips, her cheek streaked with hair moistened by saliva, the deep, sheltering cavities at her collarbone, those beautiful breasts. . . He muttered, 'The hell with it,' and gathered her up in his arms.

Dave Tucker had pulled rank. Donna and Sheena had been given a shared room, and communal nookie was no one's idea of fun. It was a cold night, but Vinny and Sheena, equipped with a double sleeping-bag and a duvet, had been billeted on the verandah.

The cold had its advantages, Vinny had to concede. Such as, for example, that Sheena clung to him like gum. They lay there, snuggled up and gazing up at the night sky.

'Vinny?' Sheena's voice was small. 'What's the name of my constellation, the one I like?'

'Orion,' Vinny whispered.

'Where's it gone? I can't see it.'

Vinny pointed. 'There. Look.'

Sheena sighed as though *that* was all right, then. She laid her cheek against his chest. 'Vinny?' she whispered again, 'Do you love me?'

He grinned down at the top of her head. 'You know I do. I'm mad on you.'

'Mad? Mad mad?'

'Dead mad.'

Sheena smiled happily and kissed his left pap. 'Vinny, I want to have a baby.'

'Yeah?' Vinny's broad grin and the tightening of his grip on her shoulder belied the casualness of his tone. 'What for?'

'Well, I don't know. I want someone to wear our colours, fly our flag for us, you know?'

Vinny pursed his lips and mused. 'Yeah,' he said at last, 'Reckon I can buy that.'

She raised her head at that and looked down at him, and she looked inexcusably lovely with a quicksilver aura of moonlight. 'You can?' she squeaked.

'Course I can. World needs more little girls like you.'

She kissed him very slowly, and once more curled up in his arms. 'And boys like you. When, then?' she asked.

'Just as soon as you stop taking them pills.'

'Yeah, well. . .' She went all coy. 'Matter of fact. . .'

'Yeah?'

'I chucked 'em down the bog this morning.'

'You did? You mean. . . You mean, we may have been. . . You mean, I mean, you could already. . .'

'I *could*, yeah. I mean, it's not likely, first shot, but yeah.'

Vinny sighed for sheer happiness. 'Know

something?' he said, 'When I'm ninety-four and have prostate trouble and weepy eyes and have to get round on a zimmer-frame, I'm going to look back on tonight, and you here in the moonlight, and I'm gonna think, "I've got no reason to complain. I've really been lucky." If's its a girl, we could her Stella, for the stars. If it's a boy. . . How about Orion Bowles?'

She giggled. 'Orion Bowles. Silly bugger. I don't think he'd thank you.'

'Maybe not. Here, Sheen. . .'

'Hmm?'

'Stands to reason, doesn't it? More shots you have at the target, better chance you've got of hitting the bull, right?'

There was a long silence, broken only by the shrieking of some night bird. 'I suppose that's right,' Sheena said at last.

'Reload,' murmured Vinny as he rolled over and nuzzled into her throat. 'Ready! Rapid fire. . .'

She squeaked and laughed. 'Mmm,' she groaned, 'Not too rapid. . .'

Donna and Dave had a relationship like the little girl with the curl. When it was bad, it was horrid, but, when it was good, it was very, very good. Making up almost made the rows worthwhile. Tonight, they had made love with a hunger bordering on ferocity. Now, sated and happy, it was playtime. For the benefit of Paddy and Nancy next door, Dave bounced on the bed and slammed the bedhead against the wall while Donna whooped and moaned and giggled.

Love was on Paddy's mind, but Nancy was too preoccupied. Sex and worry did not mix where she was concerned. She wanted this great stubborn ox of a man to talk to her, to discuss the pros and cons of her promotion. He wanted to ignore it like a headache, hoping it would just go away.

For the moment, she was seething about Tony Wilton. *That* did not make her feel exactly sexy either.

'. . . getting his end away with some Kiwi scrubber!' she said over the banging from next door. 'I mean, it's absolutely inexcusable. What the hell are we supposed to say to Joy?'

'Nothing,' Paddy shrugged.

'Nothing?' Nancy frowned as though the thought were freakish. 'God, I couldn't even look her in the eye. I almost wish I didn't know. It just gets me so worked up . . .'

Paddy came up behind her. He mumbled, 'Nancy . . .' Strong arms encircled her. One large hand gently cupped her right breast. His lips were on the nape of her neck, her ear.

She was rigid. 'Oh, come on, Paddy,' she sighed,

and sidestepped from his embrace. 'Please.'

'What? What's wrong?' Paddy was all injured innocence. 'We haven't been together for two weeks. God, I normally have to fight you off.'

'Yeah, well.'

Next door, Donna released a shriek. The banging grew faster. Paddy called, 'Take it easy, Dave. You've got all night!'

'No, come on, Paddy, seriously, please,' Nancy perched primly on the edge of the bed. 'I really need to talk to you.'

'What is there to talk about, for Christ's sake?' He flung himself down on the bed beside her and rolled over as though to sleep.

'I've got to talk to you about. . .'

'Your bloody promotion. Yeah, well, I don't want to talk about it. You know how I feel.' He raised his head to roar to Dave and Donna, 'Shut up, will you?'

'Paddy,' Nancy spoke into the echo. 'I haven't got long. . .'

'Yeah, well, you needn't think that I'm going to rubber-stamp some scheme that's going to tear us apart, because that's what this'll do, Nancy. There'll be separate postings. We'll never get to see one another. . .'

'Look, Paddy; I'm not going to be just another typical army wife like poor Joy. I've got a job to do and I'm good at it. . .'

'Sure, and I've encouraged you, haven't I? Everything's fine as it is.'

'But you can't stop the clock, Paddy,' Nancy wailed, 'Things move on.'

'Why?'

'Because that's nature.'

'Doesn't have to be. You're a human being. You can choose. Look, I've told you. I don't want to talk about it.'

'But it *matters*, Paddy,' she pleaded. She wanted to hit him, to pick him up and shake him. This was her career, her life that they were talking about. . .

'No,' Paddy's voice was muffled by the pillow. 'Our marriage matters. That's it.' Again he raised his head and bellowed to the couple next door, 'Will you bloody shut up!'

Donna and Dave cackled. Paddy covered his head with a pillow. Nancy closed her eyes and muttered prayers, profanities or a mixture of both. She kicked off her shoes, switched off the light and lay down for a night which, she knew, would be sleepless and loveless.

Chapter 8

'Let's assume that the enemy's dug in. . .'
Osbourne indicated a point on the contour map
in the HQ Ops. 'What would you do then,
Kieran?'

Kieran Voce squinted into the bright morning
light. He moved round to see better. He folded his
arms. 'Hmm. . .' He considered. 'Under those cir-
cumstances, I'd order my mortars to fire all four
tubes to soften up the enemy position here. I'd
then want to capture this bit of key terrain here.
That would allow me. . .'

'Excuse me, Colonel.' James Mercher broke in.
He laid down the telephone receiver.

'Yes, James.'

'Major Colin needs to confer about the
artillery fire plan.'

'Right,' Osbourne picked up his cap from the
table. 'No, Kieran, your plan's fine in theory, but
remember, the reality is going to be quite different. We've got a few surprises up our sleeves. Be
alert.'

He tucked the swagger stick under his arm and
marched briskly to the door.

James Mercher, who had begrudgingly accepted the role of safety supervisor for the exercise, still retained his arrogant and somewhat bullish manner. He sauntered over to Kieran's side. 'I'd recommend two tubes only,' he drawled. 'Four would be like using a sledgehammer to crack a nut.'

'Well, when I need an opinion on that,' said Kieran stiffly, 'I'll confer with Captain Phillips.'

'Just sharing my experience with you,' said Mercher. He spoke very softly, but his tone was not appeasing.

'Yes, well, I'd rather you'd run through the various safety acts for the mortars and artillery and when they're going to switch fire.'

Mercher gritted his teeth and exhaled noisily. 'They'll switch when you get to this line. . .' he pointed, 'which I'd advise you to reach within the first hour.'

Kieran sighed. 'James,' he said, 'the timing of this attack is my responsibility and mine alone.'

'Look,' Mercher barked. He thrust his face forward until it was inches from Kieran's. 'You can timetable the exercise any way you bloody like, but just remember, today you are absolutely dependent on me, as safety supervisor, for information. Can you handle that?'

Kieran met the other man's gaze. He nodded slowly. One corner of his mouth curled up in a quizzical, humourless smile. 'I have no problem,' he said. 'The question is, can you?'

Live ammo, like hanging, concentrates the mind wonderfully. There was a bustle about the camp that morning. Soldiers ran this way and that. Officers strode from building to building, supervising loading, running checks on vehicles and weapons. The shouts of CSMs and the answering cries of 'Sir!' rang in the air.

For all the work, the word went round the camp like a pox. Not only had Tony been caught *in flagrante* by the girls last night, but this morning a Kiwi sergeant had had to collect him from Ellie's house because he was late on duty, and Tony had brazened it out, giving her a long, lingering snog right there on the stoop, in full view of the street.

Vinny did not care. Vinny was too generally chuffed with life to care about anything. Sheena loved him, he was going to be a dad and there was the prospect of rare sport today. He sang as he went about his business. Midnight told him to pipe down, but he was too full of it.

Paddy Garvey, by contrast, had a right royal cob on. He knew that he was being unreasonable but could see no way out of this situation. He would not speak because he could not. All the emotions which he was feeling were nowadays considered improper, but he nonetheless felt them. He wanted Nancy to be there for him. She was the mainstay of his life. Yes, he knew that that was selfish, that the notion of a helpmeet was out of date, maybe unfair, but a helpmeet was what he needed.

Tony's indiscretion contributed to his anger. It was sloppy and bad for morale, but, more to the point, Paddy was irritated to see a man with a good, loyal wife chucking it all away for the sake of a bit of rumpy-pumpy, when Paddy would have given almost anything to keep his own marriage on the rails.

He bawled Vinny out, therefore, for dropping a crate of ammo at the rear of the truck, and got a good dig in at Tony whilst he was at it. 'You treat live ammo like you would a member of the female sex, Vinny – gently and firmly. And be bloody careful it doesn't blow up in your face,' he said pointedly.

Tony got the message. He walked briskly over and pushed Paddy in the chest. 'Let me tell you something, Paddy Garvey,' he said. 'I'm getting a little bit bollock-bored with all this "we're in the Army, we're your family, brothers-in-arms" horseshit.'

'Oh, is that right?' Paddy nodded.

'Yeah. That's right.'

'Yeah, well, loving wife and beautiful kid

114

aside, all this is turning you into a lousy soldier,' Paddy told him. 'You were late on duty today and your mind's not on the job.'

'You want to watch it, Corporal Garvey,' Tony snapped.

It was not Paddy's morning for backing down. 'No, you watch it. The girls have got no divided loyalties on this one, Tone. Soon your bit on the side won't be the only one who knows the score.'

'Ah, bollocks,' Tony sneered. He strode off, rapping out orders with more assurance, Paddy reckoned, than he possessed.

Vinny either did not notice this exchange or pretended not to. He continued to heave crates of ammo into the truck. 'It's my first time live firing, this,' he told Dave and Midnight.

'Yeah?' Dave was absent. He had paid close attention to the tiff between Paddy and Tony. He reckoned he'd be well-advised to avoid both of them for the time being. 'Yeah, so how come?'

'I had glandular fever last time.' Vinny jumped up on to the truck.

'Oh, aye, mononucleosis, the kissing disease.'

'Yup. In your DIY medicine manual, is it?'

Dave smiled. 'Shut it, smartarse.' He too jumped up and took his seat. Midnight clambered up behind him. Paddy pushed up the tailboard and shot the bolts.

'Get some cam on, Corporal Garvey!' screamed Tony as he marched to the cab.

Midnight whistled silently. 'Gor. I wonder how late he was up last night.'

'Yeah,' said Dave, 'and how far.'

'I don't give a shit who was what, up where, where he put it.' Paddy scowled. 'Just shut up, right? I'm knackered and I'm pissed off.'

'Sleepless night, was it, Paddy?' Dave grinned.

Paddy cast him a glance that had been dipped in curare. 'Just shut up, Dave' he warned, and strode round to the driver's seat.

He climbed up to find Tony scribbling on a scrap of paper on his knee. He glanced down at the heading before turning the ignition key. 'Writing a letter, are we?'

'No, boiling an egg.' Tony was sour.

'"My darling, I think". Smashing, that is. Could mean anything, couldn't it?' Paddy pushed the lever into first gear. He put his foot down and the truck jerked forward at the head of a column.

Tony folded the paper and thrust it into a pocket. His mouth was a thin, straight line. 'It could be to anyone, Corporal Garvey.'

'Yeah, and you couldn't give a toss, could you?'

'Not about what you think, no,' shouted Tony above the roar of the engine. 'Right, let's concentrate on this exercise, shall we?'

*

116

'Thanks for coming, Ma'am,' Nancy told Kate Butler. Both women laid mugs of tea down on the blue formica. 'I didn't know if I should ask you.'

Kate looked out through the canteen window at the column of trucks moving out, plumed with dust. She sighed. 'It's nice to be in demand. So,' she brightened, 'I imagine Paddy's giving you grief over this career move?'

'He won't even discuss it with me, and I don't want a fight. God, he can be so frustrating!' Nancy reached in her bag and pulled out a packet of cigarettes. 'God, I mean, I don't smoke, but I've been doing twenty a day.'

'I suppose there's no point in my saying that it must be very difficult for him. I mean, he's been twelve years in the Army, and a first-rate soldier, and he's still a corporal.'

'Yeah, but I don't think it's that. I think he's proud of that bit. He's always encouraged me. No, it's the separations. I mean, he's got a point, but I really, really want to do this job. I'm not ready to just settle down. . .'

'You'd like to put marriage on hold for a few years?'

'No!' Nancy slumped. 'Well, yes, I suppose.'

'But he's older than you and wants it to evolve. You're both in the right of it. That's what makes it so difficult.'

'Are you saying I should never have married him?'

Kate laughed. 'There'd be no point, would there? You did, and we're here and now. We've got to move forward, not worry about hypothetical situations. Fact is, you weren't fully aware of what marriage entails.'

'No, no, it's not that.' Nancy exhaled twin columns of smoke. 'I love Paddy to bits, Ma'am, and I knew what marriage meant. My mam was a devoted wife all her life, though dad was impossible. What I didn't know was how much I'd love my work, how – well, I was useless when I started, but I'm really good at it now. I've got – I don't know – an instinct for it. It'd kill me to give it up now.'

'And he won't talk?'

'Not a word. He sees me as conspiring to bust things up.' Nancy wearily shook her head. 'I just want him to approve, to egg me on, say, "Go for it." Give me permission, I suppose. Pathetic, eh?'

'We all need encouragement, Nancy.' Kate laid a long hand on the other woman's forearm. 'But your troubles won't be over when he gives you the thumbs up, you know. Being a female achiever ain't all it's cracked up to be.'

Nancy started, frowned. Here was an attractive, successful female officer questioning the joys of success. 'Why?' she asked. 'In what way?'

Kate sighed. Again her eyes wandered to the window. 'Where do I start? Resentment? Restrictions? Underestimation? I mean, suppose Paddy can't match you rank for rank? Need I go on?'

'No.' Nancy stubbed out the cigarette. She raised a hand to her brow. 'Please don't.' She set her jaw. It was not as impressive as a similar gesture from her husband, which had been compared to a rockslide on Mount Rushmore, but this jaw, if smaller, had a firmness of its own. 'But I want to be a sergeant, Miss Butler. And I want a commission too, eventually.'

'Well, good for you,' Kate smiled, 'But do you want it enough?'

'What? Can I take the pace, you mean?'

'Oh, I have no doubt of that. No, that's not the problem.' Kate drained her cup. 'No, every moment is an exchange of the past for the future. How much are you prepared to give up to get what you want? This is what you've got to decide, Nance. How much can you let go?'

The three girls lay flat on their backs on Nancy's bed, soothing swollen eyes with cool cucumber slices. 'Sacred shrine?' Sheena giggled. 'Never been to one of them before. Will it be interesting, d'ye reckon?'

'More interesting than sitting about this camp, any road,' Donna droned.

'And at least it's free,' added Nancy.

'Might prove more expensive than you've bar-gained for,' Donna grinned.

'How's that?'

'Well, 'cording to Don, it's supposed to have a magical effect on a woman's fertility.'

'Yeah?' Sheena was glad that the others could not see her. She tried to make her voice sound casual. 'You have to do anything special, then?'

'Oh, aye,' Donna was the instant expert. 'Me, I'll be walking around it with my eyes closed and my fingers and legs well crossed. The Kiwi lasses as want bairns walk round the thing three times, wave their hands above their heads in salutation to whatever gods are there, then pinch a handful of soil and sleep with it under their pillows. Nine months later – well, I suppose they have to do the business and all – nine months later, they're up to their elbows in baby food and shitty nappies.'

'Oh thanks, Donna,' Sheena laughed, 'Trust you to make it sound lovely and romantic.'

'Babies?' Donna hooted, 'Lovely and roman-tic? You're doolally, you. Months of waddling around with a coal-sack attached to your belly, a few years of sleepless nights, no nookie, no time to yourself and constant worry, then, just when they're getting to be able to take care of them-selves, they up and kick you in the teeth.'

'Yeah, well, it won't be like that for Vinny and me.'

'Oh, yes, it will, hin. Make the most of your days of freedom. If you get a touch of the broodies, come down to Macaulay's childminder's and see the little darlings in action. That'll cure you.'

'Yeah, well. . .' Sheena's lips twitched. 'I have got the urge, actually, and so has Vinny. . .'

Nancy lifted the weight of her trunk on to her elbows. She relaxed one cucumber disc. 'Hey, you mean. . .?'

'Yep.' Sheena nodded smugly. 'We're gonna have a baby.'

'Sheena, that's great,' said Nancy with genuine warmth. 'When's it due?'

'Well, it isn't yet,' Sheena admitted. 'Not yet. When I say, "We're gonna have a baby," I mean we've started trying.'

'Well, don't hold your breath,' advised Donna, unimpressed. 'It took our Shelagh four years to get in the club.'

Nancy once more subsided on to the bed. 'Still, I think it's great you're going for it,' she said. 'I'm not ready, me.'

There was silence then, save for the slow woofing of the fans.

'Can it really take years?' said Sheena at last.

'Oh, yeah,' Donna was again the expert. 'Longer if you do it standing up.'

121

Nancy frowned. She turned her head towards Donna, then a nasal cymbal clash heralded a incredulous giggle. She let the cucumbers drop from her eyes, squeaked 'Donna!' and reached for the nearest pillow to chuck.

This was when soldiering was fun. This was what all the training had been for – when adrenalin was squirting like a warm whisky hit through every vein, when all personal differences were subsumed in the spirit of the group, when you acted and reacted in a sort of trance, but acted and reacted right because training told. In this state, you could almost admire yourself as you might admire another good soldier, so little did you – the conscious you – consider what the next move should be.

And then, Paddy thought as he flung himself flat behind Tony in the scrub, there was that extraordinary joy and sense of power which sprang from trust in your mates. Where one man was vulnerable, a platoon, a troop, a regiment like this, united in pursuit of one end, seemed invincible.

'Right, listen up.' Tony was consulting the map. He panted between phrases. 'That is our main objective, OK?' He pointed first at the map, then at the hill above them. 'So we'll be left flanking along this gully over here. Number One platoon will give covering fire from that ridge over there. Got it?' He directed the question to the platoon commanders. Paddy and Dave both nodded. 'Right.' Tony wiped his moustache on his sleeve. 'We are not home to Mr Cock-up, gentlemen. And remember, the 570 rule applies at all times. Make sure you're prominent. I don't want any of you silly bastards getting shot. Now, prepare to move and – go!'

Paddy led his men at the double up to the ridge. He appraised as if by reflex as he ran the enemy positions above. It was already getting hot up there. The dust spurted into unseasonal, short-lived flowers as bullets struck. The rat-a-tat and the ragged chorus of shouting was the soundtrack to a hundred vivid memories of Goose Green, the Gulf. . .

'Yeehah,' Vinny whooped as the platoon once more fell prone. A broad grin painted a diamond on his face.

'Steady up, there, Vinny,' Paddy snapped. 'There's a hell of a long way to go yet. Right, there they go. Rapid fire, go!'

The guns bucked and spat. Beneath and behind them, Kieran Voce crouched, watching, hands over his ears. Dave knelt with the mortar. A Kiwi soldier dropped in the shell. Dave fired. The hillside splashed. You could feel the tremor from here. Again the mortar boomed. Again the land above the enemy position erupted. 'Right lads!' Paddy roared above the rattle , 'We'll be going fast to the first bit of cover. Keep your heads down, and remember, spread out!'

Vinny winked at Midnight. Paddy studied his watch. Twice more the mortar roared and the shell whooshed and whistled, then Paddy was up and shouting, 'Move! Move! Come on!' And they were off and running.

And again came the order, 'Down! Rapid fire!' And again the men fell forward, and again the gun-slings rattled and the guns shuddered, then again, 'Prepare to move! Move! Move! Come on! Mooove!'

The shrine was an oasis of peace – the sort of thing that Donna, at least, would have associated with Japan rather than with New Zealand. There was a spring which fed a gently babbling stream; there were weeping willows and chinking birds. Many of the rocks scattered about the gardens were carved with whorls and chevrons which had a Celtic look. There were votive offerings, too, many of them centuries old – bows, bones, animal skulls, bowls wrought in stone and, of more recent date, crude paintings and even photographs of babies.

'It's lovely,' said Nancy.

'Yeah, really peaceful,' Sheena agreed.

'Odd, that,' Donna had to put the dampers on their reveries, 'I mean, this is meant to be about fertility, right? And usually fertility means bloody frantic activity and moaning and groaning, then bloody frantic activity and bloody screaming nine months later. . .'

'Donna. . .' Nancy chided.

'. . .and no sooner have you stopped screaming than the sprog takes over. So what's with all this peace and tranquillity, like?'

'You're a poet, Donna,' said Nancy.

'So spiritual,' Sheena nodded.

'Well – I mean, no. I'm not objecting to a bit of peace and quiet. Lord, no. Grateful for any chance I can get. After a Dave and Donna special or a couple of hours with our Macaulay, I can see the attractions of silent orders of nuns. Sit there, watching paint warp, no men, no kids. . .'

'Ah, come on,' Nancy grinned, 'You a Poor Clare? I can just see it. You're not so bad at breaking the peace yourself, Donna. And you love Macaulay really. Don't you miss him?'

Donna cocked her head to consider this. 'Mmmyes,' she said, then shrugged. 'I dunno. I thought I'd miss him more, leaving him with my mam like this. . . I mean, yeah, I do miss him, but. . . I dunno. I feel like I've got my own life back since I've been here. You know, the hitching, the time alone with Dave. I feel a bit like a teenager again, which means I feel like a grown-up again, if you see what I mean.'

'Course I do,' Nancy sighed. 'You give up a lot when you have kids. I don't know. Maybe I'm spoiled. I mean, I'd like my own one day, but I can't imagine... I couldn't, not yet. Here,' she turned, 'Sheen, what you up to? Come on.'

Sheena had been crouching some ten yards back. Now she straightened with a smile. Her purse was in her hand. 'Just dropped my money,' she said, 'Got to look after every last cent.' She clicked the purse shut.

Neither Donna nor Nancy saw that what she had dropped into the purse was not coins but soil.

Atlas had the shakes. The whole earth was jiggling. It was like hand-held 35 mil, only somehow, under the helmet's rim, it was wide-screen. Kieran Voce was up there with them now, driving into the cover of a scrubby tussock along with Paddy and Dave, Tony, Midnight, Vinny, the whole crew. They had made good progress.

'So far, so good, Kieran panted. 'OK, Sarn't Wilton?'

'Sir,' Tony nodded and gulped air.

'Right.' Kieran narrowed his eyes as he gazed up at the enemy position. 'Come on. Section One, prepare to move! Move!'

'Dave!' Paddy bellowed and indicated with his arm. 'Take them up the side!'

And again they were running, crouched, IWs at the ready. Kieran watched them go. His eyes flickered this way and that, seeking danger.

Eight hundred metres up on the hill, danger lurked unseen.

'Cover!' Paddy had roared, dropped and rolled before he had fully registered why. The dirt was spitting as tracer rounds swept across the scrub just feet away.

'Christ!' Paddy yelled, 'Where the hell did that come from? Anyone know where that came from?'

The whole platoon scanned the hillside. It was Vinny who caught a glimpse of a movement up to their right. 'Corp!' he squealed in excitement. He raised his head and pointed. 'I've got it!'

Paddy crawled across to him on his belly. He looked where Vinny pointed. 'Good lad, Vin,' he growled, 'but keep your bloody head down, will you, man? Stay down, lads.' Paddy signalled to Dave up on the hillside. Both men pulled out thunderflashes and lobbed them up at the enemy ambush. Four men emerged from their hiding-place, hands held high.

'Nice one, Vinny,' said Midnight and reached out to touch his friend's arm.

Paddy was busy with the field glasses. 'Yup,'

he said, 'Enemy position 100 metres further over the hilltop.'

'Right.' Tony beckoned for the RT. 'Yankee Zero Alpha,' he rapped, 'this is Yankee One Zero Bravo. New enemy position 100 metres forward over estimated position.'

Kieran's voice came crackling over the RT. 'This is Yankee Zero Alpha. Roger. Wait.' There was a moment's silence, then, 'Yankee One Zero Bravo, this is Yankee Zero Alpha. Take position. Go firm. One platoon give fire support.'

'Roger. Out.' Tony laid down the RT and addressed the men. 'Thompson! I want you covering that ridge fire support, OK? Garvey, left flanking along this gully, assault section, OK? Got it? Happy? Go! Go!'

'All right lads, listen up.' Paddy shouted to his platoon. 'We're giving the left flank an assault down this gully. Thommo's giving fire support. Prepare to move and – follow me!'

Kieran was hard pushed not to punch the air and say something like 'Wayhey the lads' when, ten minutes later, he received the signal that his men had crested the hill and were looking down on the enemy position. In his first command, victory was within his grasp and, thus far at least, there had been no cock-ups. He had ordered ten mortar rounds fired at the enemy in order to soften them up. If James thought that that was using a sledgehammer to crack a nut, too bad. Kieran wanted this nut smashed to smithereens, and he'd take a steamroller to it if necessary. Now Kieran counted as the mortars whoomped and boomed. 'Seven. . .eight. . .nine. . .'

'Ten.' said the Kiwi officer.

'What?' Kieran turned his head.

'Ten rounds, Sir.'

'I only heard nine.'

'How many did you count?' Kieran asked another New Zealander.

'Ten, Sir.'

'Damn it.' Kieran frowned and winced. He chewed on his index finger. 'I'm not happy. Something's wrong. . ..' He strode over to the RT operator. 'Give me that,' he ordered curtly. 'This is Yankee Zero Alpha,' he snapped, 'Hold positions. I repeat, hold positions. . .'

It was an agonizing minute before the RT rasped into life again. 'Voce, this is Mercher. Why has this advance been checked?'

Kieran was shaking his head, bewildered, as he answered. 'I can't account for all mortar rounds.'

'Have you checked with the mortar line?'

'Yes,' Kieran sighed unhappily, 'They counted ten. I'm not sure. . .'

'Yes, well, while you dither around, this entire exercise is collapsing.'

Kieran looked heavenward for inspiration.

None was forthcoming. Every eye was on him. Everyone was waiting. Up there on the hill, the soldiers had the scent of victory in their nostrils. They would not thank him for snatching it from them. On the other hand, if there was an unexploded mortar round out there. . .

'Are you prepared to give the command?' Mercher's voice was scornful.

'I'm still not sure. . .' Kieran now gnawed his lower lip.

'*Will* you give the command?'

Kieran struggled, but the pressure was overwhelming. 'All call signs,' he said wearily, 'this is Yankee Zero Alpha. Resume advance.'

'Thank you,' Mercher snarled sarcastically.

Up on the hillside, Paddy whispered 'Yes,' then called, 'Number 13, prepare to move! Move! move! Go! Go! Go!'

They streamed down on to the plain in waves. Dust and smoke obscured all but your nearest neighbours as you ran forward, fell flat, gave covering fire, moved on. . . This was the infantry equivalent of the cavalry charge, the descendant of the thin red line, the steady, mechanical, barnstorming assault protected by a constant curtain of fire. Any enemy who raised his head must have it blown from his shoulders. Here was the intoxicating thrill of battle which, in the real thing at least, must be replaced by the horror of defeat, the

130

brutal facts of victory. There was Dave yelling, 'This is bloody fantastic!' There was Vinny, beaming all over his face, going too fast, damn it. . .

'Slow down, you bastard!' Paddy roared above the gunfire, but Vinny had lost it, was way ahead as the rest of the line went down. 'Vinny, get down!' Paddy yelled, 'Get down, get down!'

Then Midnight was off after him, Paddy up on one knee in hope that he could bring the rogue cog back into place in the machine, and suddenly a geyser spurted from the dry earth and the shock waves knocked Paddy back and the explosion came to the ears, as it always did, after the damage was done.

'Shiiit!' Tony Wilton was up and running past Paddy now, heedless of his safety, and Paddy was on his feet and lumbering towards the spot. There was screaming in there amidst the smoke and the drifting dust. Dave was in there, shouting, 'Vinny, Vinny, you mad git, what are you playing at, eh? Vinny? Christ!'

Paddy stumbled over Midnight. Paddy held up the black man's head. The eyes were wild, the face coated with grime. There was heat and moisture somewhere beneath Paddy's left hand. Dear God, thought Paddy, let it be his arm not a gut wound. He held up four fingers and bawled, 'How many fingers, man?'

'Four!' Midnight groaned.

'Say it again!'

'Four! Four!'

'Is he all right?' Tony's voice at Paddy's shoulder.

'Yeah, he's all right.' Paddy nodded. 'Arm injury. Dave. Help Dave.'

Through the smoke, he could see Dave kneeling, could hear him gabbling, 'Pulse, pulse! Give me your pulse, you tight little bastard!'

'For Christ's sakes, Dave, give him some morphine!' Paddy called across.

'I can't, you twat! He's got a stomach injury. Vinny!'

Tony knelt beside Dave. He breathed. 'Jesus!' and Paddy knew then that it was bad.

'He's got a pulse but he's not breathing, Tone. He's not sodding breathing!' Dave almost howled. 'Where the hell's the MO?'

'He's on his way, he's on his way. Give him mouth to mouth or – or something.'

'His throat's blocked. Can't get air down. He needs a bloody tracheotomy!'

'So give him one!'

'I can't. I'm only trained in immediate first aid.'

'Shit!' Paddy saw Tony reach into his pocket. A moment later, a penknife glinted in his hand. Tony leaned forward. Dave winced. 'Get a tube out of the bag!' Tony ordered. 'Give it here. Right, do exactly as I tell you. . .'

Suddenly Midnight writhed and moaned, 'Where's Vinny?'

'He's all right,' Paddy lied. 'Don't worry. That's not your snooker arm, is it?'

'Vinny!' Midnight was not to be fobbed off. 'Vinny!'

'He's all right, he's all right. . .'

'. . . Hold it there,' Tony was saying. 'All right? You got it? You OK?' and Dave was crooning, 'Good lad, Vinny. There's a boy,' as he might to a dying dog.

At last came the sound of a siren. In common with anyone else who has lived in a city, Paddy had come to hate that sawing sound in the Hong Kong nights, yet now it seemed sweet music. The field ambulance jerked to a halt. The MO was out of it before it had stopped moving. The orderlies followed with stretchers.

'Severe abdominal,' Paddy heard Dave mumble, 'given him a tracheotomy.'

'Thank you.' The MO was brisk and calm. He reached for the radio mouthpiece in his ambulance. 'Get a chopper in here now,' he ordered. 'We need to get this man to general hospital.' He marched over to Paddy. 'Your man?'

'Arm badly wounded,' Paddy reported. 'Don't know if there's anything else. There's a lot of blood, but he seems OK.'

'Right. We'll take over. . .'

Paddy and Tony reeled away from the carnage. Dave stayed in there, crooning reassurances to his friend, the man with his head in his lap. Paddy just caught a glimpse of Vinny's face as he passed. It was white as a cloud.

Paddy lit two cigarettes and handed one to Tony. All differences were forgotten now. 'Well done, Tone,' he said, 'I'm impressed.'

'I saw a feller do it in the boxing ring once. Swallowed his tongue...' Tony spoke in a drunkard's dreary monotone. 'Swallowed his tongue...'

Paddy tried to get things back to normal, but he knew that they would never be back to normal again. 'The lads are all over the place,' he said.

'I'm all over the place,' Tony confessed, and slumped to the ground.

The two men watched with dull, staring eyes as the helicopter descended, the stretcher-bearers loaded up their two mates, and Dave, trying to board with them, was gently pushed back. Dave stood alone and forlorn, hands hanging useless and empty by his sides, as the rotors spun and the helicopter once more took to the skies.

Paddy walked over to Dave. He laid a hand on his shoulder. He said, 'Bloody hell, mate,' which did not mean a whole lot, but wasn't far from the truth.

Dave just nodded slowly.

Suddenly Tony was back with them – not the Tony of a few minutes ago, but Sergeant Tony Brisk-and-Bristling Wilton. 'Right, come on, come on, get a grip! We've got two injured men. It happens. We are not going to go to pieces, are we?' This evoked no response, so he bawled in Dave's ear, 'Are we?'

'No, Sarge,' said Dave, and Paddy felt the shoulder beneath his hand rising.

'Tucker, there is blood on your face. Remove it at once!'

Dave nodded and reached for a handkerchief.

The Wilton line in condolences might never be a starter in the greetings cards class, but it worked.

If there was stillness now on the ground where there had been feverish activity, the formerly calm helicopter was now a battlezone. Midnight lay on one side of the chopper, unable to move as they washed and dressed and bandaged his shattered arm, whilst over there, they attached drips and monitors and God knew what to the ashen, unmoving body of his friend. Midnight hardly felt his own wound. He was concerned about just one thing. 'Vinny?' he kept moaning, but all anyone would say was, 'It's all right, mate,' just like that lummox Garvey, when Midnight could see clear as day that it was anything but. He just did not know what questions to ask. His brain was still spinning from the blast, so it just came out as 'Vinny? Vinny?' and the answer came back again and again like a distorted echo, 'It's all right, mate. It's all right.'

And suddenly even that consolation was gone.

'He's arrested!' shouted the doctor at Vinny's head, and even the guy treating Midnight rushed over to lend a hand.

'Vinny?' Midnight bleated, but they were too frantic to heed him.

'...starting CPR...' he heard, and did not know what it meant, didn't need to know. He'd heard the desperation, the urgency in the voice.

'Vinny?' said Midnight, and tears filled his eyes.

'One thousand, two thousand, three thousand, four thousand, five thousand...' an orderly counted, and there was a strange macabre bouncing sound.

'Vinny? Vinny, hold on...'

'One thousand, two thousand, three thousand, four thousand, five thousand...'

'Vinny...' Midnight's call ended on a little whiplash sob.

'One thousand, two thousand, three thousand, four thousand, five thousand... No. It's no good. Tell the pilot to forget about the hospital.

There's nothing they'll be able to do. Call the senior MO and advise him.'

And suddenly the man who had been dressing Midnight's wound was back there, winding the bandages about his elbow. 'Is that it?' Midnight squeaked. 'Is that all you're going to do?'

'I'm sorry,' the man said with a slow shake of his head. 'That's it. No, lie back, please. We've done all we can, I'm afraid. Did he have a family?'

'Yes,' Midnight blurted, and a huge sob burst from him. 'He's got a wife. He's got a wife...'

Donna clattered into the camp's canteen. 'Over here, Sheena, pet,' she pronounced. 'I'm going to give you some money for the bandit, see if you can pump up the spends.'

Sheena giggled. Nancy was, as ever, the sensible one. 'Here, Donna, come on. We can't afford to gamble.'

'Oh, straighten your face,' Donna was disdainful. 'This kid's magic.' She pumped five dollars into the machine and stood back to let Sheena press the buttons. 'Her luck, we'll all be treating the lads to a steak dinner and champagne tonight. She wins plane tickets, wins at the bingo. Fruit machines are child's play to the likes of her. Her number's on it, up it comes.'

The reels whirred. There were three clunks.

The machine suddenly started pumping out coins. And continued to do so. And continued.

Sheena squealed and jumped up and down in a dance of triumph.

Nancy screamed, 'I don't believe it!'

Donna chortled. 'What did I tell you?'

And still the machine continued to spew forth the precious coins which now tumbled on to the linoleum floor.

All three girls were hopping about and screaming by the time the machine finally decided that it had paid out enough. All that remained now was to bend down, giggling, and to fill their hands with all that lovely money.

It was Nancy who first raised her head to see Kate Butler standing in the doorway. Then Donna, her hands dripping coins, said, 'Lovely grub,' straightened and clocked the look on the family officer's face.

'. . .I mean, how much is all this in English?' Sheena crowed. 'Maybe, way my luck's running, I should put it all on a horse or something. . .'

'Miss Butler,' Nancy said softly.

Sheena turned her smiling face towards the doorway. And knew. 'Not Vinny?' she said in a small voice, and the coins cascaded from her hands.

Chapter 9

'Once in a blue bloody moon it happens,' Mark Osbourne said from between gritted teeth. 'As if there weren't enough analysis and scrutiny coming up in any case with the amalgamation looming. Why this exercise? Why now?'

'It might sound better,' Ray Curry reproved, 'if you were to say, "Why him?"'

Osbourne nodded. He was pacing in front of Curry's desk. Now he pulled himself up short and stopped to consider. 'Yes, of course. You're absolutely right. It shouldn't happen to any soldier in peacetime. Not under my command.'

'Ah, it's not your fault,' Curry cheered him. 'There are many more fatalities on building sites. Still, there'll have to be a full enquiry.'

'Of course. You'll be presiding?'

'Yes. Yes, as CO, I feel I must. Of course, this will only be a preliminary board – very informal.'

'Right. No, I understand. . .' Osbourne stopped at a rap on the door.

'Come!' called Curry.

Kate Butler marched into the room. She

saluted both men. 'I'm sorry to disturb you,' she started.

'Not at all, Kate,' Curry smiled his lopsided smile. 'Do you want to speak to Colonel Osbourne privately?'

'No, that's fine, thank you, Sir. I've just been to see Sheena Bowles.'

'Ah, good,' said Curry. 'How is she?'

'Bad, Sir. We've moved her into the spare room in the hospital wing as you suggested, Sir, and the other girls are doing their best to console her, but it's no easy job. She's very young, and her Vinny was her whole life.'

'I understand that,' said Osbourne.

'The thing is, Sir,' Kate swallowed, 'She's requested to be allowed to identify the body.'

'Yes?'

'Well, he was wearing his ID,' Kate shrugged, 'so I told her there was no need. . .'

'There's Sheena's need, Kate.'

'Yes, Sir. . .' Kate hesitated. 'Look, Sir, I seem to have been landed with the Families Officer job. That's fine, but it means that I'm responsible for Sheena and – well, frankly, Sir, I don't know how to help her.'

'This whole business is very difficult for all of us,' Osbourne sighed.

'And it is only twenty-four hours, Kate,' Curry reminded her. 'She's got to go through the grieving process. Until that's done, you know, there's not much any of us can do.'

'No, but – I don't know. I'm supposed to be good at this because I'm a woman, but frankly, I'm all at sea.'

Osbourne nodded. 'Fair enough. Dealing with death isn't easy for anyone. Do you want some help, Kate?'

And Kate Butler steeled herself to say the hardest thing of all. 'Yes, Sir. I do.'

Kieran Voce marched up to James Mercher in the billiards room of the officers mess and announced, 'We've got to sort this out, James.'

Mercher potted a green with unnecessary violence. He straightened to appraise the next red. 'It's out of our hands now, isn't it?'

'Yeah, well, sure, we'll both have to make statements, but we've got to talk about it. . .'

Mercher brushed past him and leaned forward to address the cue ball. 'There was an unexploded mortar round,' he said with an implicit shrug. He doubled the cue-ball back to pot the red. 'So what is there to talk about?'

'Listen, Bowles was running way too fast,' Kieran persisted. 'He completely disregarded Garvey's orders. If that mortar had gone off when it was meant to, he wouldn't have been anywhere near it.'

'Yeah, but he was.'

'We should never have carried on with the attack.'

'You mean, I suppose,' Mercher at last turned away from the table. He held the cue across his chest like a quarterstaff. He sneered, 'I should not have insisted that you continue?'

'No!' Kieran protested. 'No, look, no one's to blame. No one person, anyway. I'm not obliged to take orders from you. I should have stood my ground.'

Mercher reached for the whisky tumbler on the corner of the table with a hand that trembled perceptibly. He drained the glass in one. 'Just why are you doing this?'

'What?'

'This special pleading bit, this no one's to blame stuff.'

Kieran's hand went to his brow as though to still a clamour in there. 'It keeps going round in my head, that's all.'

'Yeah, I bet. Awkward thing to happen at this crucial stage in the rise and rise of Kieran Voce, isn't it?'

Kieran's jaw dropped. He could not believe that the man could think like that. 'I don't give a toss about that,' he said.

'Oh, so it's my career you're worried about? Sweet of you.'

'What?' Kieran was confused. James Mercher came, it seemed, from a planet wholly alien to his. 'Look, we're in a team, right? We're in this together.'

Mercher picked up his empty glass and flung the cue down on the baize. 'Thank you, but I'm quite capable of looking after myself,' he spat, and strode from the room.

The body was only a body. It was not a human being. It had nothing to tell Sheena except that Vinny was truly and totally gone from her. The face without animation was not his face, nor the tapering fingers that she had loved his fingers. This was a waxwork, a vestige of Vinny altogether less evocative than the photos, even the clothes, the books. They spoke of what Vinny had been, of his enthusiasm and his tastes. This body spoke of nothing save absence.

It was strangely consoling for Sheena to know with certainty that Vinny was gone from this, his former home. There had been, perhaps, some lingering hope that all this had been a terrible joke or a mistake on the part of the doctors, that he might awake with a characteristic laugh or a silly joke on his lips, but no laughter would again move this anonymous amalgam of flesh and bone. Sheena was not a religious person, and had no idea where Vinny might have gone, but one thing was clear. He was no longer known at this address.

'I suppose – I'm so used to his being away,' she told Kate and Osbourne as they left the mortuary, 'You know, training weekends, border patrol, all that, some part of me kept thinking he's be coming back with the chocolates and the dirty washing, you know? Like he always did. Now I know. Thank you for showing me.'

'Um. . . No. . .' Osbourne pushed open a swing door into a waiting room. 'While you're here, perhaps we can sort out a few details, if that's OK?'

Sheena shrugged. 'Sure.'

'Do, please, sit down.' Osbourne indicated a scarlet banquette. 'Can I get you something? Tea? Coffee?'

'No.' Sheena sat decorously. 'No, thank you.'

'Now,' Osbourne leaned against the drinks dispenser. Kate took her place on the banquette beside Sheena. 'Did you want Vinny's body taken home to England?'

'I don't know.' Sheena's wide eyes were dark with weeping and rubbing. They stared through Osbourne. 'What does the Army usually do?'

'Well, in peacetime, in cases like this, the funeral usually takes place in England. As the next of kin, however, the decision is of course yours.'

Sheena nodded. 'Best do it here, then.'

'You're sure now?' asked Kate.

'Well. . .yeah.' Sheena sniffed. She waved a hand as though to indicate the whole of New Zealand. 'I think it's meant, you know? You see, I won these travel vouchers to come here. I wouldn't have been here if he was meant to buried in Hong Kong or Oldham.'

'No,' said Osbourne, who did not seem convinced. 'Umm. . .'

'I was wondering if you'd like to lay a wreath on the coffin,' put in Kate.

'What. . .?' Sheena's voice faltered. She looked from one officer to the other. 'What does a soldier usually have?'

'Just his beret,' said Osbourne.

'No flag?' She was desolate, as though the flag mattered more than anything else at that moment.

'Oh, yes, yes,' Osbourne was quick to reassure her. 'Yes, a flag, of course.'

'That sounds lovely.'

'Very well. Splendid.'

'Er, would you like me to talk to the padre about readings?' Kate asked.

'Please, can we have something not out of the Bible?' She was decisive about this. 'Can we have a poem?'

Osbourne raised his eyebrows. 'Did Vinny like poetry?'

Sheena nodded. 'And the stars.'

'Ah,' said Osbourne. 'Well, I'm sure we can find something suitable, eh, Miss Butler?'

'I'm sure we can.'

'Colonel Osbourne?'

'Yes, Sheena?'

'If you don't mind, I'd prefer if it was something that didn't mention soldiering.' Sheena caught the exchange of glances between the two officers. 'I don't mean. . . I mean, the army was very important to Vinny, the regiment, all that, but that was. . . There was so much more to him.'

'I understand exactly,' Osbourne nodded. 'Don't you worry now, Sheena. We'll organise everything.'

'Can I. . .' Sheena started, then, 'Well, if it's possible, I'd like to see Midnight.'

'Midnight?' Osbourne frowned.

'Fusilier Rawlings,' supplied Kate.

'Ah, yes. Yes, of course. Listen, if you'll excuse me now. . . All right with you, Kate?'

'Yes, Sir. Of course.' Kate stood. 'And thank you, Sir.'

Osbourne nodded once and marched from the room.

'All right, Sheena?' Kate asked as the echo of her CO's footfalls died away.

Sheena nodded. 'You start out saying, "This is so crazy, it must be a dream," and if it's a dream, you're going to wake up, aren't you? That's why I needed to see it. Now I know it's not a dream. It's just crazy.'

'It's horrific. It may be no consolation right now, but at least you know that he died doing what he loved best, surrounded by his friends and knowing that you loved him. We've all got to go, but to do it in hot blood and in those circumstance. . .'

'Yeah.' Sheena got up very quickly and took a preternatural interest in the text on the drinks dispenser. 'Yeah. No, you're right. He's OK. It's us selfish sods left behind have a problem. Funny.' Her shoulders rose and fell. She sighed. Her voice was suddenly very high-pitched. 'I keep thinking, "why couldn't it have been Paddy Garvey or Dave Tucker?" I mean, Vinny was so *young*. And then I feel all dirty and guilty for thinking it. And Donna and Nancy say they spend all the time feeling guilty because it wasn't Dave or Paddy. Like I said, it's crazy.'

'It's grief,' Kate put her arm round Sheena's shoulders. 'Surviving is the tough bit. Come on. Let's go and see Midnight. And remember, he was there. He survived too.'

'Here you go, mate.' Paddy thrust a folded wad of notes at Dave. 'There's a ton. Best I can do.'

'Nice one, Paddy.' Dave took the money and

147

thrust it into the drawstring bag. 'Right, guys. Come on, cough up. As much as you can.' He moved on round the groups of men and women scattered about the parade ground.

'Hiya,' said Nancy at Paddy's shoulder.

He turned and took her in his arms. The scent and the warmth of her embrace was a momentary relief from all the horror and sorrow.

'Is that a whip-round for Sheena?' Nancy asked over Paddy's shoulder.

'Yeah,' Paddy sighed. 'I don't know. Dave seems to think he could have done more for him. One way or another, everyone's trying to take the blame.'

'Oh, Babe, I am sorry.' Again she kissed him and hugged him tight.

'Better watch it, you,' Paddy growled. 'You're only here on compassionate grounds. You look like you're enjoying yourself, you'll be on the next flight back to Hong Kong.'

'Yeah. Right. Listen, Paddy, can we sneak off somewhere? We really do have to talk.'

Paddy set his jaw. 'Do we?'

'Yeah, I go back to Hong Kong on Friday. I want all this sorted.' She was very serious. 'I have to get my acceptance for the sergeant's course in.'

'I told you,' Paddy strode off towards the camp gates. Nancy had to put in two strides to every one of his. 'It's not even something I want to talk about.'

'Paddy!' Nancy stopped. She caught two invisible cannon balls. She trembled with frustration. 'Look, my career matters!'

'Nope. Our marriage matters. I told you. It matters even more after all this. After Vinny. At least, it bloody well should do.' He glared back at her. 'Ah, hell,' he snapped and flapped a dismissive hand. 'Sod it. I've got work to do.'

'Oh, yes,' Nancy ground her teeth as he stormed off. '*You've* got work to do. And me? And me?'

'Midnight?' Sheena tiptoed into the ward as though sound could damage broken limbs.

'Hey.' Midnight turned his head and afforded her a grin like a Cadillac radiator. He saw Kate Butler in the doorway. He raised his right hand in a half-hearted wave. 'Sheena, listen, I'm so sorry.'

Sheena sat on the bed. She leaned across to kiss him. 'I'd get a card,' she said, 'but I haven't seen a card shop. You should have something on your locker.' She fell silent then, her tiny hand in the huge cigar-case of his. 'Er. . .' she said, even as he said, 'Um.'

'Go on,' she smiled.

'No, you.'

149

'I just wanted. . .' Sheena glanced over her shoulder. Kate was busy studying her nails and trying very hard to evaporate. 'I mean, you were with him.'

'Yeah. To the end.'

'Did he. . .? Did he say anything?'

'Yeah. All he said was, "I'll be OK, but, if not, make sure you tell Sheena I love her."'

'He. . .?' Sheena gulped. Her eyes shone.

'He really did,' Midnight assured her.

'What? Love me or say so?' She essayed a giggle. It came out as a croaked sob.

'Both,' said Midnight, and his hand tightened about hers. 'He told me a lot, Sheena. . .'

But it was too much for her. She squeaked, 'Sorry. . .' pulled her hand from his and ran for it. Kate Butler held out a hand as she passed, but Sheena brushed it away. 'Sorry. Please.' She heaved up a lungful of breath. 'Let me be. . .'

Kate sighed and nodded as she watched her go. She knew that Sheena was undergoing a necessary and natural process. She also knew that she would come through it all in the end. Kate wandered into the room and sat at the foot of Midnight's bed. 'Thanks,' she said.

'Ma'am, I was lying.'

'Yes,' Kate smiled. 'I gathered that.'

'I mean, he couldn't speak at all, with his throat and that.'

'No. I know. Don't worry. I won't tell her.'

Midnight shifted uncomfortably on the bed. He looked down at his hands. 'I mean, what it really was, I was being selfish really.' He raised his eyes to the ceiling. They were oily with tears. 'I mean, if it had been me, I wouldn't have been able to say I loved someone, because I don't, and there'd be no one there to tell about it, no one there to cry like that.' Twin giant tears spilled from his eyes and wriggled down his cheeks. He wiped them angrily away on his sleeve. His voice emerged as a sort of honk. 'It really pisses me off, Ma'am. I mean, he had Sheena. He was going to start a family. He told me. I mean, why...? If it'd been me, it wouldn't have mattered...'

'No, no,' Kate laid a hand on the weeping man's giant forearm. 'You mustn't think like that. You have a future. You'll have a family. You'll find someone to love you. It's an accident of fate that it happened to Vinny, but you mustn't hurt yourself for still being here.'

'I just miss him!' Midnight blurted. 'Like I said, it pisses me off...' Sobs shook his frame. He raised a hand to cover his face. Again, then, he looked upward at the light and blinked and sniffed. 'I won't be... I won't even be able to carry his coffin.'

Kate Butler shook his arm. 'There'll be

something for you to do, Rawlings,' she said. 'I promise.'

Tony Wilton should have felt great. He had made love with a beautiful, sinuous, smooth-skinned, uninhibited woman who now lay curled in his arms. He had dreamed of such luxury, had watched the movies, thought, 'God, I could use that' – uncomplicated affection, uncomplicated sex, unburdened by all the emotional baggage which encumbered his relations with Joy. And here it was.

He felt lousy.

He felt itchy, too, nervous, eager to be up and out of here. Her skin seemed to cling to him.

He said, 'Ellie. . .'

And she, nestling in closer, 'Mmmm?'

'You know I care about you, don't you?'

She very suddenly rolled away from him. She spoke to the wall. 'You're going to end it, aren't you?'

'No. . .I just. . .' It was difficult to find words because he knew that half of him, at least, would regret this. 'It's just that. . . Well, I've been, you know, thinking a bit recently.'

'Because of the man that got killed?'

'Well. . .' Tony struggled. A blue light swung about the darkened room as a car sped by. 'In a way. I mean, I've been thinking about my kid without a father, you know? I mean, lately I've been losing it a bit.'

She sat up now, drew her knees up to her breasts and clasped her feet. 'What are you talking about?' she asked, but she did not turn to face him.

'Well, you know, my sense of what's right. . .' It sounded so pompous, so pi. 'In the army, you know, it's important, what's right. I've been losing a lot of people's respect. My mates – they've been shutting me out. . . Ellie, I can't live out on a limb. I need to belong.'

'Yeah, tell me about it.' Her chin was on her knees now, so her mouth barely opened. 'Out on a limb. Yeah, you should try it some time. It's a different world.' She threw herself back in bed and turned her back to him. 'Look, will you just get dressed and go.'

'Don't be like that, please, Ellie,' he said, but he swung his feet from the bed and reached for his shirt.

'And don't you act like you're the only one to say it's over,' she sneered. 'You're not the only fish in the sea, Tony Wilton.'

For a moment the thought of anyone else here, easing her loneliness, caused a pang of pain and regret. 'Ellie, please. . .' he said, wanting her to make it easy, knowing that her pride could not permit it.

'Yeah, and don't expect me to beg you to stay.'

'No.' He hastily pulled on his trousers and slipped into his shoes. Every rustle of fabric seemed loud, intrusive, intimate. 'No. Right, well. . . Sorry.'

He looked down at her, at the glow of her skin, and seaweed fronds of dark hair, and he knew that this was a farewell, not just to Ellie but to all she represented. He sought reassurance. 'Did I. . . Did I make you happy?'

'Not really.' She pulled up the sheet. 'Had a bit of fun, I suppose.'

'Right.' He leaned over to kiss her, but she stiffened. He straightened and backed to the door. 'Sorry. See you. . .'

He felt bad as he shut the front door behind him, then he took a deep breath of the cool fresh air and could have danced in his relief.

Chapter 10

'Yes, Sir,' Paddy told the board of enquiry the following morning. 'The men crossed the line at 0900 hours, Sir.'

Curry nodded and jotted something on the tablet before him. 'And was this as laid out in the battle plans?'

'It was, Sir. On the dot, Sir.'

'How would you describe Fusilier Bowles's demeanour at the time of the attack?'

Paddy plucked at the hackle on the beret in his hands. He considered. 'He was excited, Sir.'

'Over-excited?'

'Yes, Sir.' Paddy was definite. 'He was a natural enthusiast and this was his first live firing exercise. He was going a lot faster than I'd have liked.'

'He was out on his own?'

'Yes, Sir. In the region of twenty metres ahead of the rest of his fire team, Sir. Just before the explosion, Fusilier Rawlings ran forward. I formed the impression that he was trying to check Vin. . . Fusilier Bowles, Sir. Rawlings was shouting. He came to within about five metres of Fusilier Bowles.'

'Yes,' Osbourne was also making notes. 'Rawlings has confirmed your impression. He was trying to bring him back.'

'Thank you, Corporal,' Curry smiled reassuringly.

Paddy stood, replaced the beret and saluted.

He marched into the fresh air of the parade ground to find Nancy waiting for him. She looked angry. She fell in beside him. 'Well, we're off tomorrow, after the funeral. So do I go off to London without our ever having talked about it properly?'

'What's all this going off to London bit?'

'That's what I'm going to do, Paddy.'

Paddy gazed heavenward and breathed a silent prayer which didn't sound terribly pious.

'Ah, come on, Paddy,' Nancy groaned. 'You encouraged me before. You told me it was a good idea to go for promotion.'

'Sure,' Paddy acknowledged the truth of it. He had encouraged her, but that was when it had just been a joint game. Now it was serious. 'Sure, hold on, hold on. . .' He winced and covered his face with his hands. It was doing his brain, this. He wanted just to be able to say, 'What does your poxy work matter?' He wanted to be able to say, 'I'm engaged in tough, unrelenting work and I want my wife to come home to at the end of the day.' He wanted to be able to say, 'Why can't you just have babies? Damn it, Donna's done it. Why can't you just have babies and look after me instead of playing at soldiers?' But those words were not permissible, and he didn't even mean them, not in his head at least, but in his heart. . . Well, his heart was unreconstructed.

'So didn't you mean it?' Nancy demanded.

'Yes! No. Not this way. Not without discussing it properly.'

She stopped and stared. 'Paddy, how can you? Why do you think I came here? All right, this Vinny thing, sure, it knocked everything sideways, but don't tell me that you've been listening and I've been refusing to talk. I've tried and I've tried.'

'OK, OK. Right.' Paddy walked sulkily on. 'I'm listening now.'

'Look, Paddy,' Nancy sighed. 'I've rung and accepted the place on this course. I had to let them know today.'

'Oh, great!' Paddy laughed without humour. 'So I was to get back from New Zealand, find you already gone, is that it?'

'Paddy, this is important to me? Can't you help me?'

'Important,' Paddy spat. 'So important that you just walk out on me. You weren't even going to tell me. You were just going to go.'

'Look, we're talking a ten week course, for God's sake, not a bloody lifetime.'

'Yeah? And then what?' They were out on the country road now and well out of earshot of the camp, so Paddy gave vent to his feelings. 'You won't stop there, will you? You said so yourself. You said, if it goes well, you'll go for a commission, and you know what that'd mean.'

'We're not there yet, Paddy,' Nancy soothed. 'I'm not walking out on you. I just want this opportunity and I'm asking you for your support. We'll take it stage by stage.'

'Yeah, well I'm not sure that I want to. . .' Paddy lengthened his stride so that she could not keep up with him without running. He paced on, head down. She stopped and stood watching, her mouth as tight as a mussel's shell.

The tribunal continued its enquiries. Now it was Tony's turn.

'In your opinion, Sarn't Wilton,' said Curry, 'did Corporal Garvey take the appropriate action?'

'Absolutely, Sir.' Tony was prompt and certain. 'He shouted to Fusilier Bowles to stop, but – well, I assume that he didn't hear him. It was a very noisy day, Sir.'

'Was there any way that he could have been stopped?'

'Not from where we were, no, Sir. Rawlings tried, but that meant breaking ranks. It would have been disastrous if Corporal Garvey or any of the others had done the same thing all for one man.'

'Quite so,' Curry nodded. He turned with a quizzical look to Osbourne. Osbourne too nodded.

'Very well, Sarn't,' said Curry. 'Thank you.'

'Oh, and well done with the tracheotomy,' added Osbourne. 'The MO tells me that you did exactly the right thing and did it well. That took courage, Sergeant. I will file a commendation for your prompt initiative.'

'Thank you, Sir.' Tony allowed himself the luxury of a smile as he wheeled and made his way out through the crowded anteroom. He was back on track, back where he belonged.

'Yeah, OK.' Paddy sat on the hilltop, plucked grass and threw it angrily away. 'So it's a great chance for you, but where does that leave me?'

'It needn't affect you.' Nancy shrugged. 'Why should it?'

Paddy stared. 'Am I going mad? Or is it you?'

'What do you mean?'

'You don't see it, do you?' he shook his head in bewilderment. 'You become a sergeant, fine. That's not the problem. The problem is that you won't stop there. You'll carry on, and end up at Sandhurst for a year, and then you'll get posted to God knows where. I mean, what'll happen to our family, eh? Where are the kids? They're just going to pop out on your days off, are they?'

There it was, the admission that his biological clock was shrilling even if hers was not.

'Oh, come on, Paddy,' Nancy chided sympathetically. 'I'm twenty-five! I've got years before I need to think about all that.'

There was silence then, because there was nothing to say. There was no compromise possible. She wanted one thing, he another, wholly incompatible. Neither had chosen this conflict, but each was keenly and stubbornly aware that this was the only life that each was going to get, and that they were discussing the whole shape of these lives. Paddy gave it a try nonetheless. 'Oh, come on, love,' he sighed. 'Come here.'

She shuffled sideways and leaned tentatively back in his arms.

'I don't want to make things difficult for you, Nance, love.'

She sniffed. 'No. I know.'

'I mean, we should be making plans together. . .'

'That's what I want.'

'Well, we'll sort it all out when I get back to Hong Kong, have a really serious look at it. . .'

'Paddy. . .'

'I mean, this isn't the only sergeant's course. . .'

'No, Paddy!' she yelped, and span to face him. 'I am going on this course.'

'Christ!' Paddy roared. He leaped to his feet. 'One extra stripe on your arm, one poxy stripe on your arm is worth more than our marriage, is it?'

'No, Paddy,' she closed her eyes. They were back where they had started. And she was not going to concede.

'Captain Voce, what led you to suppose that one of the mortar rounds had failed to detonate?' Curry asked.

Kieran appraised the question for a minute. 'It was just. . . I don't know. There was a cluster of explosions and I couldn't be sure how many I'd heard. I thought it was nine.'

'And did you confer with anyone?'

'Yes. Yes, I did. Everybody else thought that they had heard ten. If I'd stood my ground, we'd never have messed up.'

Curry was stern. 'It isn't up to you or me to decide who's responsible, Captain Voce. We're here to gather the facts and made a formal recommendation. A final verdict is in the hands of a full Board of Enquiry.' He leaned forward on his desk. 'Now, given your reservations, how do you account for your conduct?'

161

Kieran shifted uncomfortably in his chair. He pursed his lips.

'Well?' Curry prompted at last.

'Captain Mercher insisted that I continue, Sir.' Kieran spoke softly. 'As I say, I should have stood my ground.'

'Thank you, Captain Voce.' Curry leaned back and again released that 1,000 megawatt smile. 'If you would be so kind as to ask Captain Mercher to step in. . .?'

The fight had gone out of Paddy Garvey now. He had recognized that the lady was not for turning. He had fought many an enemy, but never one that he loved. That tied your hands. Nancy and he had walked back in silence to their allotted room in the camp. Now he sat on the bed with a bottle of beer in his hands and stared morosely at Nancy's back as she packed.

'So where does this leave me?' he spoke in a voice like a muffled drum.

'That's up to you, Paddy.'

'Is it?' he tipped up the bottle and gulped. He gasped. 'You're the one who's pissing off to London.'

Nancy hit the folded clothes. She sighed. She walked slowly over to where Paddy sat. She placed her palm against his cheek. 'Oh, God, we've made a right old mess of this, haven't we?'

162

Paddy shook his head to slough off her caress. 'First hurdle we come to, we fall flat on our faces.'

'We don't have to.' Paddy blinked. The alcohol and the caress were too much. The tears were hot in his eyes. His voice faltered. 'I love you, Nancy, and I want you with me.'

'Yeah,' Nancy nodded. 'On your terms.'

'No. . .no. . .' he shook his head fast. 'No terms.'

Her smile was despairing. 'Sez you,' she said.

'Yeah. . .' His shoulders slumped. 'Yeah. Sez me.' He flung himself back on the bed and drank deep.

'I am sorry to have kept you waiting,' Curry told Mercher. 'Please sit down.'

Mercher removed his beret. 'Right. Not at all, Sir.'

'Now, were you ever aware at any time that there was a possibility of an unexploded mortar round?'

Mercher's neck expanded twice. 'I was, Sir.'

'Hm. How were you made aware of that?'

'Captain Voce informed me that he could account for only nine.'

'Yes?' Curry's voice was mellifluously coaxing. 'And what action did you take in consequence?'

Mercher's jaw worked. 'I – I overruled him, Sir. I advised him to get on with it.'

163

'And did you give him that advice directly?'

'Yes, Sir.' Mercher croaked. 'I didn't think he was doing the job properly. I was. . .' he gulped and started again. 'I was wrong.'

Curry cut through the self-abasement. 'Did the mortar platoon commander or any other of the safety staff share Captain Voce's doubts?'

'No, Sir. They all heard ten.'

Curry nodded. Osbourne nodded. 'Thank you very much, Captain Mercher,' Curry said smoothly.

'But that's not the point,' Mercher blurted. . . 'Sir,' he added.

Curry started. 'Sorry?'

'The fault was mine,' Mercher raised his chin as though proud of his guilt. 'I should have supported Captain Voce in his suspicions. I was aware only of being able to prove a point.'

'Captain Mercher. . .' Osbourne leaned forward to check the confession.

Mercher swept on. 'You see, I resented being taken off my mortar platoon. I was desperate for a chance to assert myself, and everything that happened after – the death, Rawlings's injury, everything – was because of my stupidity. I just wish you'd called me in sooner. It would have saved a lot of unnecessary questioning of other people who were blameless. I don't want anyone else held responsible for Bowles's death.'

'Ah,' said Curry.

'Oh, hell,' murmured Osbourne.

'Thank you,' said Mercher. And was gone.

Paddy Garvey hardly felt the weight of the coffin on his shoulder. It amazed him that in there, just inches from his head, there lay a man who, just days before, had been full of fun and vigour. It was as though that personality had had substance and mass. In death, Vinny was light as a child.

And now he was at peace. Paddy almost envied him as he, Dave, Tony Wilton and the other pall bearers slowly led the long procession of mourners through the leafy churchyard to the site of the grave. Vinny had no further worries, no further aspirations, ambitions, fears or frustrations. It was over. 'The day thou gavest, Lord, is ended. . .', they had sung at the service. Night-time sounded good.

'One thing you can say for the army,' Dave had told Paddy out of the side of his mouth this morning as the funeral party prepared to move out. 'They give you a bloody good send-off. May treat you like dirt when you're alive, but, you get killed, you get the flag, the salutes, the works. Ten years from now, in civvie street, you'd get the missus and the priest and two paraffin lamps from the pub hoping for a free drink. Here, the whole camp shows up, Colonel, Kiwis, the whole lot.'

Paddy had nodded agreement. It was true. Vinny was being seen off in style. Every badge, button and buckle glittered. Every toe-cap was a morion mirror. The brass were there in the full scrambled egg. A soldier had died – one of their own. He would be afforded a soldier's honours.

They had also sung *Abide with Me* and the little church had shaken as though in an earth tremor. Paddy had afforded particular feeling to the lines, '*Change and decay I all around me see;/Oh, Thou who changeth not, Abide with me*' Midnight had sobbed openly. Even Dave had discovered something in his eye and had had to rub it away. As for Paddy, out and out grief and pride were such simple emotions that they came almost as a relief after all the confusing, conflicting feelings of the past few days.

The Fusiliers laid their fallen comrade's coffin by the side of the grave. They took one pace back and stood to attention. Sheena, pale as the moon in her black dress and coat, took her place at the graveside, flanked by Donna and Nancy. Osbourne, grave and grand, stood behind her. Kate Butler was on hand, as was Kieran Voce and the bloody Mercher, who had the grace to look gutted. Then came the rest of the Fusiliers, executing a perfect slow march to come to a stamping halt, then the black-clad Kiwis. Many of them would never have known Vinny, but they were soldiers. It could have been them. They gave such honour as they would hope for themselves.

Midnight stepped forward. His arm was in a sling. The snail's trail tracks of tears glittered on his black cheeks. His reading was not fluent. It stopped then started as he gathered breath or fought for control over his quivering voice, but it was nonetheless affecting for that.

Remember me when I am gone away,
Gone far away into the silent land,
When you can no more hold me by the hand,
Nor I half-turn to go, yet, turning, stay;
Remember me when no more day by day,
You tell me of our future that you planned;
Only remember me. You understand,
It will be late to counsel then or pray,
Yet, if you should forget me for a while,
And afterwards remember, do not grieve,
For if the darkness and corruption leave
A vestige of the thoughts that I once had,
Better by far you should forget, and smile,
Than that you should remember and be sad. . .

Hearing Rossetti's words, Paddy thought that Vinny had said it all in his own words, in his own

way: . . . *My light*
Might
Mean Something to
Somebody,
Somewhere in time.

'Forasmuch as it hath pleased Almighty God of his great mercy to take unto him the soul of our dear brother here departed. . .' intoned the padre. The Fusiliers bent to pick up the straps and slowly, with as little rasping as possible, lowered the coffin into the cold red loam.

And it was done, and once again they stood back to attention, and behind them, the King's Fusiliers raised their rifles and fired into the air, and the echoes fluttered in the trees like the birds which arose at the sound. Then it came, the final farewell to every man and woman in arms, the last post until the very last trump of all. Everyone saw Sheena drop earth on to the coffin-lid, before turning into Nancy's embrace, but only those up front saw that the dirt came not from the earth at her feet but from a woven purse which she carried between her hands.

It was a day for farewells. No sooner was the funeral done and lunch picked at by an entire regiment which had mysteriously lost its appetite than the Land Rover for the girls' return journey drew up outside the main door.

It was all right for Donna and Dave, Paddy thought. They might live life on the edge, always making up and breaking up, but look at them now, snogging like teenagers on a first date, for Christ's sakes, whilst he and Nancy stood shuffling on the steps with two foot of air between them which might as well have been six foot of cold marble.

'So, you're set on it, then?' Paddy asked.

'Paddy, I've got to,' Nancy grimaced.

'Yeah. . .' Paddy blinked up at the clouds. 'Right. . . So, what. . .?' he stopped because his voice had skidded alarmingly upward. He swallowed, put on the brakes. 'So what happens after the course? You stay put, right?'

Nancy shook her head hard. Her fist hit her right hip. 'I don't know, Paddy. I don't know anything yet.'

'You do know,' he croaked.

Kate Butler had escorted Sheena into the vehicle. A soldier had thrown the luggage in the back and was shooting the bolts on the tailboard. Even Donna had put Dave down and was clambering into her seat. The driver started the ignition.

'Look, I'll call you.' Nancy stood tiptoe to afford him the lightest of kisses. The rims of her eyes were filled with tears. 'See you,' she breathed. She turned away.

169

'Nancy. . .' he held out a hand, but already she was clumsily climbing up, averting her eyes from everyone's glance. The driver thrust the gearstick into first. Donna was supplying a chorus of 'ta-ra chucks' which sounded like a farmyard impersonation. Nancy kept her eyes on something in the distance on the other side of the vehicle. She was rocked backward, then forward as the Land Rover moved.

'I'm gonna miss you, Nance!' Paddy called. Then the car was gone, and Paddy plunged blindly back into the building in search of the privacy of the loos.

It is not to be wondered at, then, that, for their several reasons, Paddy, Dave and Midnight got quite seriously drunk in the Hot Lava that night, nor that, when Dave called out, 'Oi, oi, oi! A toast, ladies and gentlemen!' and everyone fell silent, he should raise his glass and announce, 'Absent friends!' It should be no cause for surprise, either, that the King's Fusiliers, to a man, repeated these words with solemnity and drank deep, nor that Paddy spoke them a little later than everyone else, and with a particular pensiveness.

BROOKSIDE FROM THE INSIDE

The dramas, the traumas, the good times and the bad

BETH JORDACHE: THE NEW JOURNALS,
0 7522 0765 2, £4.99 pb
* Following on from *The Journals of Beth Jordache*, Beth intimately reveals her relationships with her family and her fears for the future
* Focusses on the year leading up to Beth's imprisonment and tragic demise

DAVID CROSBIE'S MEMOIRS, 0 7522 0172 7, £4.99 pb
* Urban warrior David Crosbie is the self-appointed protector of Brookside Close
* David Crosbie has been a constant source of support to Rachel during the past turbulent year

THE JIMMY CORKHILL STORY,
0 7522 0846 2, £4.99 pb
* This is the story told by Jimmy Corkhill himself
* After a shady history, have his experiences taught him enough to keep him on the straight and narrow?

THE EARLY YEARS, 0 7522 1051 3, £7.99 pb
* Featuring all your favourite characters past and present in full colour
* Chronicles the show and includes profiles of cast and characters and plot summaries

LIFE IN THE CLOSE, 1 85283 954 6, £9.99 pb
* What happened where: maps and diagrams to show where important incidents have happened
* Who lives where: names and addresses of everyone who has ever lived in Brookside Close, packed with colour photos

ORDER FORM

SOLDIER SOLDIER

☐ 0 7522 0755 5	Damage	£4.99 pb
☐ 0 7522 0230 8	Starting Over	£4.99 pb
☐ 0 7522 0750 4	Tucker's Story	£4.99 pb

BROOKSIDE

☐ 0 7522 0765 2	Beth Jordache – The New Journals	£4.99 pb
☐ 0 7522 0172 7	David Crosbie's Memoirs	£4.99 pb
☐ 0 7522 1051 3	Early Years	£7.99 pb
☐ 1 85283 954 6	Life in the Close	£9.99 pb
☐ 0 7522 0846 2	Jimmy Corkhill Story	£4.99 pb

TV HUMOUR

☐ 0 7522 0179 4	Ellen	£7.99 pb
☐ 0 7522 0184 0	Friends	£9.99 pb

All these books are available at your local bookshop or can be ordered direct from the publisher. Just tick the titles you want and fill in the form below.

Prices and availability subject to change without notice.

Boxtree Cash Sales, P.O. Box 11, Falmouth, Cornwall TR10 9EN

Please send a cheque or postal order for the value of the book and add the following for postage and packing:

U.K. including B.F.P.O. – £1.00 for one book plus 50p for the second book, and 30p for each additional book ordered up to a £3.00 maximum.

Overseas including Eire – £2.00 for the first book plus £1.00 for the second book, and 50p for each additional book ordered.

OR please debit this amount from my Access/Visa Card (delete as appropriate).

Card Number ☐☐☐☐☐☐☐☐☐☐☐☐☐☐☐☐☐☐☐

Amount £ ....

Expiry Date ....

Signed ....

Name ....

Address ....

....

....